FORWARD THROUGH THE FERTILIZER

Horse Haven: 3

G.G. Marshall

Forward Through The Fertilizer

Horse Haven: 3

By: G.G. Marshall

Released September 2017

Firelight Reads

P.O. Box 518

Herrin, IL 62948

ISBN: 978-1-945404-07-8

Dedication

This book is dedicated to my firstborn son, whom arrived in the middle of it being written. Thank you for reminding me why it's important to chase your dreams, how much family matters, and not to give up when life gets tough.

Table Of Contents

Chapter 1 ~ ~ ~ The Baby

Chapter 2 ~ ~ ~ Snake

Chapter 3 ~ ~ ~ Learning How To Wait

Chapter 4 ~ ~ ~ Old Friends

Chapter 5 ~ ~ ~ Fight Back

Chapter 6 ~ ~ ~ Ground First

Chapter 7 ~ ~ ~ Over The Phone

Chapter 8 ~ ~ ~ Tim

Chapter 9 ~ ~ ~ Waiting

Chapter 10 ~ ~ ~ Ezra's Parents

Chapter 11 ~ ~ ~ Unnecessary

Chapter 12 ~ ~ ~ Encounter

Chapter 13 ~ ~ ~ Green-Eyed Boy

Chapter 14 ~ ~ ~ Future Plans

Chapter 15 ~ ~ ~ Learning to Teach

Chapter 16 ~ ~ ~ War Captain

Chapter 17 ~ ~ ~ Quality Time

Chapter 18 ~ ~ ~ Plans

Chapter 19 ~ ~ ~ Just Here To Help

Chapter 20 ~ ~ ~ Worrying

Chapter 21 ~ ~ ~ Grandpa

Chapter 22 ~ ~ ~ Too Stubborn To Be Sick

Chapter 23 ~ ~ ~ Giddy Marie

Chapter 24 ~ ~ ~ Home and Loneliness

Chapter 25 ~ ~ ~ Kings and Diamonds

Chapter 26 ~ ~ ~ The Trail Ride

~ Chapter 1: The Baby ~

"Ruth, can I speak with you fer a moment?" Ezra's voice was soft and shaky. Reddened eyes with dark bags and a worried expression on the sweet girl's face threw Ruth off guard at first.

Ruth had woken up rather early that morning, considering the basic horse riding course her grandfather had been giving ended last Friday. It was the start of a new week and she had planned to sleep late but there she was, out in the barn at 8:30. She frowned at Ezra in concern. "Of course you can talk to me, Ezra. What's up?"

Ezra touched the edge of Ruth's elbow gently and pulled her into the nearby tack room, shutting the door behind them. Strange. Ezra turned toward Ruth and wrung her hands, swallowing hard.

After several minutes of silence Ruth decided to push Ezra forward. "What's wrong, Ez?"

"I'm not sure how tah say this," she started hesitantly. "You have to promise not tah tell anyone, you're the first person I've talked to."

"Of course," Ruth said softly. "I promise."

"I-I'm pregnant," the words came out quiet and unsure.

"What?" Ruth asked, her brain not processing though she fully understood the words. Ezra pregnant? The sweet, blonde-haired, blue-eyed, shy girl who was standing in front of her? The homeschooled Christian girl that was so quiet? It didn't make sense.

"I'm pregnant," Ezra repeated so softly it was barely audible.

"I didn't even know you had a boyfriend."

"Yeah, his name is Tim. I've been datin' him in secret because when my father met him he didn't like him. I know it seems crazy that I would date someone behind my family's back, but I couldn't help it. I wanted to be in love so bad and Tim is sweet."

Okay, wow, Ruth definitely hadn't expected that. "So, what are you going to do?"

"I don't know, that's why I wanted to talk to you. I need tah talk to someone! I need help. I don't know what tah do or where to go."

"What do you mean, 'where to go?' It's not like you're going to be kicked out of your home or something, are you?"

Ezra shrugged and diverted her eyes. "Maybe, I don't know. It certainly won't go over well."

"How far along are you?"

"About two months."

"And you haven't told Tim?"

Ezra shook her head. "I'm afraid he'd tell some of my family and I'm not willin' tah take that risk until I know what I'm goin' to do."

"Okay."

"So... help?"

Ruth was completely unprepared for such a request. And why was Ezra asking her? Ezra was sixteen, two years Ruth's senior. Ruth had never been pregnant, she didn't know what to do. Honestly, her and Ezra didn't even know each other that well, they'd just met that summer. Ruth tried to reel her thoughts in. "I will do whatever I can to help."

Ezra gave Ruth a tight hug. "Thank you."

A thought occurred to Ruth. "You aren't going to have an abortion, are you?"

Ezra pulled away slightly. "No, of course not!"

"Okay, good. So, you are going to have the baby?"

"Yes."

"Are you going to keep it?"

"I don't know." Ezra hugged Ruth tightly again. "I don't know," she said again, her voice quivering.

Ruth felt almost shaky with empathy. '*Poor Ezra.*' Ruth held Ezra tighter as she felt wetness on her cheek. '*Poor Ezra,*' she thought again. What could be done to help her?

Ruth decided the best course of action was to collect her thoughts before deciding what to do. She excused herself, asking for a moment to think, and then made her way to the hayloft. She snuggled against a haybale and closed her eyes, focusing on the situation.

What could be done? What could *she* do? Ezra had asked for help, maybe she already had an idea what she wanted for help, but what if it was something Ruth couldn't or wouldn't be able to give? She took a deep breath and forced herself to relax.

What would she do if she got pregnant and had to tell her father? *'Run away,'* was the immediate response that came to mind, but she knew that wasn't a plausible answer and dismissed it. How do you deal with a situation of that magnitude? Telling your parents about an unwed, teenage pregnancy when you grew up in a Christian home?

Ruth decided sitting in the musty hayloft, that was bound to get more humid as the Missouri sun continued rising, would only contribute to her panic. She decided instead to go for a ride, maybe a little bit of distance, combined with the calming sound of hoofbeats, would clear her head.

She headed to the tack room to retrieve a halter and lead rope, then went to the pasture.

~ Chapter 2: Snake ~

Ruth was too nervous to take Jet or Embera on the open trail, especially without someone to help or without following a more experienced horse. That left Roy and Mirage as options, and since the sheer monstrous size of the Clydesdale, Roy, left her quivering, Mirage was her choice by default.

The blue roan, part Quarter Horse mare came at Ruth's whistle with the rest of the horses following behind. Their ears perked toward Ruth, faces and whinnies expressing their hopefulness for grain.

"Sorry guys," Ruth said as they slowed upon reaching her, "I have no grain for you right now."

They didn't seem to understand but as Ruth haltered Mirage, they quickly lost interest and wandered off.

The sweet mare willingly followed Ruth to the barn. Ruth tied her lead to a wall loop and tacked her up.

As she led Mirage out of the barn, she noticed the ranch hand, Devin, mucking out a stall. She sighed in relief, she didn't want to face Ezra without sorting out her thoughts. The whole thing must be tearing the poor girl apart and Ruth was afraid her quick mouth might make things worse.

She made it to the trail and exhaled her pent-up tension as Mirage walked lazily through the trees. How was she supposed to help Ezra? The echo of Mirage's hoofbeats helped relax Ruth as she contemplated the matter.

Though she could tell the heat was only going to increase throughout the day to turn into what would likely be intolerable in the afternoon, the light breeze and shade offered by the trees made the temperature comfortable for the horseback ride. Ezra was sweet, caring, kind, determined, strong, she would find a way through this, yet it had to be terrifying for her.

The woods were beautiful and as Ruth looked at the shadow spackled ground, Ruth realized there wasn't much she could do for Ezra other than be there as a friend. She couldn't give good advice on how to handle things, she'd never been in the same situation. She didn't really know anyone else in the area so it wasn't as if she could help with reputations or had any advice on hospitals or doctors; Ezra knew those things so she must not be expecting them anyway. She must simply want a friend, someone to be there.

Ruth could do that, just be around for... Her thoughts stopped short as she noticed something wriggling on the path in front of her. A snort sounded from Mirage, her ears flicking forward, head raised in alarm. "Yeah, that's how I feel, girl," Ruth said quietly, pulling Mirage to a halt.

The nasty wriggling creature that made its way across the trail had a triangular head, a dark yellowish underbelly, and triangular-shaped, dark brown patterns across his back and sides. Ruth breathed in deep, turned Mirage around, and high-tailed it out of there at a canter.

'Ewww,' she thought with a shudder as they put distance between themselves and the serpent.

Was the creature poisonous? Dangerous? Ruth had no idea but she didn't intend to stick around and find out. She never cared for snakes. Or spiders for that matter. Or insects. Guess not everything about the country was pleasant.

As Ruth saw the clearing ahead of them, she slowed Mirage to a trot, breathing a sigh of relief at the sight of the barn. She knew the snake was far behind them but her heart hadn't slowed until she felt safe in sight of home.

Home. Was it home? She still felt Wisconsin was home, Missouri felt foreign. But it was safe enough away from the squirmy, wiggly serpent on the trail.

She rode back to the barn, dismounted in the aisle, and began to untack Mirage. Now that her heart had slowed its pounding and her hands had ceased their shaking, her thoughts went back to the matter with Ezra.

She'd made up her mind that the only way she could help Ezra was to simply keep her secret and tell her she was there to help any way she could.

As she loosed Mirage in the pasture, something else occurred to her. If it were her, if she ended up pregnant in High School, out of wedlock, the most nerve-wracking part to her would be telling her family. The fear of disappointing them, the unknown as to their reactions, would be difficult to face. Could she help someone else do that? It wasn't as if she needed Ezra's parents to approve of her. She'd like a friend there if she had to tell her family. Probably better than the boy who got her pregnant, he'd probably be public enemy number one for a while afterward. Yes, she could offer support in that way.

After watching Mirage meander her way toward the other horses, she went to find Ezra.

~ Chapter 3: Learning How To Wait ~

Ezra was moving haybales in the loft when Ruth found her. The girl's lips were tightened, her cheeks flushed, and though she looked tired and strained, she had ceased crying.

"Hey, Ezra," Ruth said quietly.

Ezra looked over her shoulder at Ruth without turning her body away from the hay she was stacking.

"Yeah?" she asked softly, returning her attention to her work.

"I just want to let you know that if you need anything, I'm here for you."

"Thank you, I appreciate that," Ezra turned toward Ruth as she finished speaking.

"I also want you to know that if you need someone to help you break the news to your parents, I'm here for you."

Ezra's aqua eyes softened and warmed slightly, she seemed truly grateful. "Are you serious?"

'No, I'm a cruel, heartless wench,' Ruth thought in response. *As if* she would joke about something like that.

"Yes, of course I'm serious."

"Wow, thank you. Thank you so much."

Ruth gaze Ezra an encouraging smile and nodded. "Of course."

"No, not 'of course.' You didn't have tah offer to do something like that." She offered Ruth a brief, forced smile. "I would like to talk to Tim first though. If he will go with me tah talk to my parents, that might be best."

Ruth nodded. She hoped Ezra was right but she wasn't sure. Would having the guy that got you pregnant there when you told your parents make it better? Would it just add fuel to the fire for a father to see the guy while finding out? Or would it be worse if he wasn't there? Would it make a father feel his daughter was knocked up by a coward?

"Thank you," Ezra said again.

Ruth realized she was standing there, just staring at Ezra while lost in her thoughts. She nodded as Ezra's quiet voice pulled her back to the present. "Well, let me know if you want me to come with you or if you need anything else."

"Okay," she said softly. "Thank you."

Ruth nodded, feeling a little awkward at Ezra's overflowing appreciation. She hadn't even done anything for her yet, she'd simply offered to be around. She bowed her head slightly in farewell. "I better be off. I want to work with

Embera some."

Ezra nodded. "I understand, I will see you later."

Ruth nodded in return then slowly made her way out of the hayloft. She was at a loss of what to say in the face of so much gratitude.

She grabbed a rope halter with a lead rope from a hook on the wall next to the tack room, something the ranch hand Devin had added recently. It was quite handy and Ruth was glad to have him and Ezra around, she wondered how much of their work would fall on her if her father hadn't hired them.

Ruth made her way to the pasture and found the horses only a few yards from the gate. She whistled and immediately Mirage's blue roan head swung up. The trusty old mare trotted over, always hopeful for treats, maybe this time as a thank you for the earlier ride she had given Ruth. Ruth wished she had brought something, but since she hadn't, she settled on scratching the mare near the top of her mane.

The other horses wandered over, except Winter's Pearl, a horse being boarded by Victoria. Jet sniffed at Ruth then the Friesian trotted off, seeming to think there were more interesting things elsewhere. Embera stayed at the back of the herd, behind Roy.

Ruth turned to the mare and smiled. She stepped

closer and Embera swung her head away, one wary eye and ear still turned toward Ruth. Ruth stepped closer and Embera walked a wide arc around the other horses so she was farther away from Ruth. Ruth sighed and tried again with a similar result.

Ruth slowly closed and reopened her eyes in frustration, letting out a loud huff.

"Didn't know ya were signin' up for a marathon!" Grandpa Malachi's teasing voice met Ruth's ears.

She swiveled around to look at the old man standing at the pasture gate. "Well, what am I supposed to do?"

"Stop rushin' things."

"And do what instead?"

She couldn't see his expression from where she was standing but she could imagine that it would be something to suggest the answer was obvious. "Take your time."

"Just stand here?" She growled back at him.

"If that's what it takes."

Ruth grunted. "Great, I'm a freaking scarecrow," she muttered. "You think she'll come to me?"

"Not unless ya stand there fer quite some time."

Ruth pinned back her frustration. "So then, what's the point of standing here?"

"Just because it will take quite some time doesn't mean it won't happen, but ya could just wait until she gets curious. Wait until she isn't turnin' her head away. Wait until she gives ya permission tah approach."

"Then she won't run?"

"Perhaps not, but don't rush it. One or two steps at a time. When she turns her head away, stop your approach and wait. It will be easier than tryin' tah chase her around, I can assure you that much."

"How can I stop catching her from being such a hassle in the future?"

"Build a relationship with her. Spend time pettin' her, scratchin' her, givin' her treats, just hangin' out. If she wants tah be with ya, she won't run away."

"And how long will that take?"

"Depends on you and depends on the horse. Stop bein' so impatient! You need horses, they'll help teach ya what holdin' your horses really means."

"Wonderful!" Ruth called to him sarcastically. *'This is going to be a fun afternoon,'* Ruth whined in her mind.

~ Chapter 4: Old Friends ~

Twenty minutes after talking to Grandpa, Ruth ventured into the house. He was right, what he'd told her to do worked, but it took a good ten to fifteen minutes for Embera to let Ruth touch her. After she finally got the mare, all she did was pet and scratch her.

She didn't know why the mare decided not to be caught, some days she just ran up with the other horses and didn't mind being haltered. Maybe that's why people called mares moody, because how much they wanted to be with humans seemed to depend on the day.

Ruth made her way to the fridge, dodging around Sophia, the bossy maid and cook, and found some orange juice as well as a cup. She poured a glass and plopped down at the table. She pulled out her cell and started to play a game on it while sipping the juice.

A few minutes later her brother David entered the dining room.

Ruth raised an eyebrow at her brother as he went past her to the kitchen. She heard some squabbling between him and Sophia. Apparently, he had not been as deft at avoiding

the woman's attention as Ruth. A few moments later he came
back and joined her at the table.

He had a box of peanut butter sandwich crackers and
a small glass of milk. He nodded at her slightly and then
started munching away.

A few seconds later he broke the silence, "What's
up?"

"Aren't you supposed to be at work?"

He shook his head, his dark brown mop hair
protesting as he did so. "You still really don't know my
schedule?"

"I wasn't aware that I had to know your schedule
because you aren't mature enough to take care of that
yourself." She was suspicious, he didn't really have a set
schedule, did he?

He rolled his eyes. "You're so lame."

"I guess I take after my older brother."

He shook his head in knowing denial. "If you really
did take after me, you wouldn't have nearly as many
problems in your life as you do."

"Oh, poke yourself in the eye, my life is awesome."

He barked an amused laugh.

"Lunch is in twenty minutes!" Sophia huffed as she
bustled out of the kitchen, carrying a stack of plates with
silverware mounded on top. "And here you kids are, ruining

your appetites!"

Ruth shared a glance with David and the bickering siblings immediately became allies. They jumped up, abandoning their posts for the safety of the living room.

They plopped down on the couch and pulled out controllers for the video game console. They agreed on a first-person shooter game and spent the next twenty minutes playing against each other, continuing their teasing until Sophia rang the triangle, signaling lunch to be ready.

Lunch was rather uneventful, just a few cross glances from Sophia that Ruth chose to ignore. After lunch, Ruth headed to her room and decided to spend some time seeing if she could find out what was going on in the lives of the friends she left in Wisconsin. She texted her two best friends, Jill and Charlene, to see what they were up to and retrieved her laptop to check social media sites.

Jill had mentioned her in a comment, saying she really missed Ruth. The thought that slipped through her mind as she read the post, was how life wasn't the same without Jill around. She realized there was a part of her that had wondered if she had made a difference in their lives at all. It was nice to be missed.

She replied to the post, saying how much she missed all of them, too and how life was different without them.

She browsed around the social media sites for a

minute then received a notification on Jill's post.

"Yeah, but you are the one that left and are getting to have an adventure!"

Ruth stared at the screen for several long moments in disbelief. Did Jill really think that leaving everything she knew, all her friends, and the place she believed her future would be, to be an adventure? A fun adventure? A willing adventure?

Sure, the horses and land were great, but would they not have been so much better in Wisconsin? Ruth sucked in a long, deep breath and then released. Jill did not mean it in a bad way but obviously she had no idea how Ruth felt about the whole thing.

Ruth took a moment to compose her thoughts then typed a response. "But you are only missing me as one friend, I am missing everyone. And my home."

A few seconds later a reply come through and Ruth clicked on it.

It was just a frowny face. Frowny face indeed.

~ Chapter 5: Fight Back ~

A knock on her bedroom door startled Ruth. "Yes?"

The door opened to reveal her father with a smile on his face. "Your friend's here."

Ruth raised an eyebrow. All her friends were back in Wisconsin, where she left them. "Who?" she asked skeptically.

"Marie. It's her first day, remember? You told her you would show her the ropes, not that I'm convinced you know them yourself."

Ruth shut her laptop as she rolled her eyes. "Believe it or not, I do work, Dad."

"I choose not to believe it, because I know you."

Ruth chuckled, getting up to follow her dad out of her room, but he turned toward his office as she headed outside.

Ruth found Marie in the barn with Ezra, who was showing her how to muck the stalls.

"Trying to pawn off the smelly jobs, I see."

Ezra looked up at Ruth, slightly hunched over the manure fork in her hands. "I am helping right beside her."

Marie looked up as well but straightened her body as

she realized it was Ruth, a beaming smile on her face. "She's been super helpful!"

Ezra looked better than she had that morning. Her face still had worry lines but her eyes and cheeks were no longer red from tears and there was even a half-smile on the poor girl's face. Hopefully she would be able to break the news to her parents soon, Ruth couldn't imagine what the girl was going through.

"I'm sure she has been, always is." Ruth gave Ezra a kind smile before her gaze flicked over to Marie. "Do you know what horse you would like to work with?"

"What are my options?" she asked with a half-frown.

"The ones from the lesson you had would be the ones you can ride. We can't let you ride the boarders' horses without their permission."

"Of course, I understand, I just didn't know if ya would have changed horses at all." Marie rocked her slightly chubby form back and forth from the balls to the heels of her feet. She was apparently having difficulty holding back her exuberance.

"Why don't you come with me? Ezra, if you want you can work on something else and Marie can finish mucking out the stalls when we're done."

A slight grin slid onto Ezra's face. "That sounds good tah me."

Ruth nodded and Marie propped her manure fork in a corner of the stall. Ezra proceeded to dump out the manure on her rake as Ruth turned and led Marie to the tack room.

"Do you remember the place well enough, or do you need a tour?"

"I think I remember it pretty well from when I took classes."

Ruth half-glanced over her shoulder and gave the girl a nod. "Alright. I'll show you how to feed horses this evening, but for now I'd like you to work with Roy if you would. I rode Embera and Mirage this morning. Unless you feel confident enough to work with Jet? Roy is better trained and has a sweet nature."

"He's so big though!"

"But he's a sweetheart. A gentle giant."

"Have you ever ridden him?"

"Two or three times."

She gave Ruth a dubious look as they collected a halter and lead rope from the tack room.

Ruth chuckled at the look. "I understand being intimidated by him, but if you're up for it, he's well trained."

Marie only shrugged in response and Ruth took that as a tentative yes.

They headed to the pasture, Marie quickly taking the lead, a bounce to her step, her nervousness overshadowed by her excitement. Ruth wondered if the girl was always that peppy or just around horses. Must be exhausting.

When they arrived at the pasture Marie let out a hearty whistle. Wow, she had a pair of lungs on her. The horses came running, all of them this time.

They began to slow as they neared the girls, all but one of them. Winter's Pearl was barreling straight for Marie and showed no signs of stopping. Her head was arched high, her nostrils flaring, her eyes wide.

A bolt of fear shot through Ruth as she reached the girl and realized they were both in harm's way. She'd never before experienced the fear invoked by a half ton animal headed straight for her, with the seeming intent to mow her down in its wake.

Marie screamed and Ruth felt her eyes bulge in fear. Her first instinct was to run but she heard a voice, almost coming from within her, telling her to "fight back." She threw her hands up, ran forward, and yelled at the mare. The mare swiveled in course, kicked her back legs out, and ran the other direction.

Ruth stood watching the mare run off, her heart beating in her sweaty palms, feeling blood coursing through her veins. She felt a hand on her shoulder and jumped. Turning, she saw Marie, her face full of concern.

"That was so brave."

"I just felt something tell me to fight back. I was terrified out of my mind."

"Something?"

"I'm pretty sure it was God."

A smile crept onto Marie's lips. "You're a Christian, too."

Ruth nodded and then took a startled half-step back as the other girl wrapped her in a hug. Ruth hugged her back quickly then wrangled free of the embrace.

Marie stepped back, her shoulder-length light brown hair falling in her face for a moment as she glanced down in embarrassment. She looked back up and said in an almost whisper, "Sorry, it's just nice tah have a friend."

'Friend? Already? We hardly know each other.' She hardly believed someone could consider her a friend as quickly as she could consider them one, usually people found her too clingy. Ruth gave the girl a broad smile. *'Thank you, Jesus.'* She knew it may seem like a small thing to some, but having a friend in the strange countryside of the Missouri hills was a true blessing to her.

To make a friend so fast was something she would have thought unthinkable, she didn't consider herself to be good at making friends. "I know how that feels," Ruth agreed. "Come on, let's get Roy ready to go." Ruth gestured toward the Clydesdale.

Marie nodded and Ruth watched the girl as she approached the gelding, put the halter on, and then turned back to Ruth. The two of them headed to the barn to get tack before moving to the arena to get the horse ready to ride.

~ Chapter 6: Ground First ~

Marie began saddling by standing on a bucket while Ruth held Roy's lead. The Clydesdale waited patiently as Marie fiddled with the girth before pleading for help to get it secured.

Ruth moved to the horse's side to help. When they finished, she showed Marie the trick of tickling the gelding's bottom lip to get him to lower his head for easy bridling access. Roy lowered his head and Marie put the bridle on.

"Why don't ya ladies start with some ground work?"

Ruth turned to see her grandfather at the edge of the indoor arena, leaning against the gate, the sun gleaming on his white hair. "Maybe I would if I knew how!" All she knew how to do from the ground was lunge.

The old man let himself into the arena, walking toward them slowly. "How long have ya been workin' with horses?"

Ruth shrugged. "It depends on if you are referring to the camps I've taken and everything, or just how long I've had horses. Because if it's the latter you know it hasn't been long."

"How about the first one?"

"Since as long as I can remember, I guess."

"And you were never taught how tah do ground work?"

"It would seem not."

"Well, why don't ya run and get Roy's halter, the rope one I had for him?" He raised an eyebrow at Ruth then smiled at Marie.

Ruth sighed, nodding in compliance before jogging back to the barn to get the halter. By the time she made it to the barn, small beads of sweat were trailing down her back. Unbelievable, Missouri heat was so intense she sometimes wondered how people physically survived.

She grabbed a water bottle from the stash in the tack room before heading back. She decided to settle for a brisk walk on her way back to the arena. The slower pace didn't help much, more sweat was dripping down her body by the time she made it back to the arena. She eagerly gulped some water down, ignoring Malachi's, "We're waitin'."

She went up to them and handed the halter to Grandpa Malachi.

"Oh, I must have forgotten tah tell ya that we need a lunge whip as well." His blue eyes twinkled.

Ruth took a deep breath, pinned him with a frustrated look, and headed back to the barn.

"I can go!" Marie called, seeming excited even about such a simple task.

"Oh no, it's fine. Ruthie doesn't mind, do ya, dearie?" Malachi said.

Ruth didn't bother turning around, just waved an arm behind her in dismissal as she continued toward the barn.

When Ruth returned, Malachi was showing Marie a place on Roy's tummy where he liked to be scratched. The horse was thoroughly enjoying himself and Marie was giggling as the horse nodded his head up and down.

"Got the lunge whip," Ruth announced from a few feet away.

Grandpa looked over his shoulder, smiled, then turned back to the horse, taking a few steps back. "Who wants tah learn first?"

"Oh me, please!" Marie giddily spoke up.

"Alright, first a few lessons in why we are doin' groundwork. Do ya know any of the reasons?"

Ruth shifted over by the horse so her and Marie could both face Grandpa Malachi while he talked. "Because it's safer on the ground than on his back."

Grandpa nodded. "What else?"

"Erm…" Marie's face crinkled in thought.

'Because you think I'm fat, and think running after a horse with a lunge whip is a good form of exercise' Ruth

joked on the inside. She couldn't think of any other reasons off the top of her head, but there must be some. Maybe? It was hard to tell with Grandpa.

"Because ya can teach the horse things from the ground, get feedback, and improve yer communication before ever gettin' in the saddle. You can test how things will work in the saddle and ya can improve yer own leadership. You can earn the horse's respect, and have him followin' ya before gettin' on his back. Then, when ya want to ride, you have a relationship established and can gauge his mood, instead of havin' an unwillin', grumpy horse."

He gave them both a few moments to think on his words then gestured at Ruth with his hand, "Go ahead and give that lunge whip tah Marie."

Ruth complied.

"Alright, now, if ya don't mind, I need ya tah back up out of the way. Maybe ya just want tah stand out of the arena for this part and watch."

Ruth shrugged, heading out of the arena.

"So, you're sayin' ya can teach the horse the things ya want tah do from the saddle on the ground?" Marie asked.

"Yeah. At the least ya can teach him the individual steps and then put 'em together on his back. If he understands what yer askin', ya might get less resistance."

"Might?" Ruth asked over her shoulder, now at the

arena's gate.

"Well, sometimes they are testin' you or your leadership, but hopefully ya can work those kinks out on the ground before gettin' in the saddle. I try tah avoid bein' bucked off, personally."

Ruth let herself out of the arena, turned, and leaned on the railing to watch Marie and Malachi. She was excited to see what was going to happen. One thing she couldn't deny was that Malachi knew what he was doing when it came to horses, it could be seen in Mirage and Roy.

Malachi showed Marie how to move different parts of the horse's body by pressing on them or pushing the air with waving hands. Then he had her and Ruth drag some things into the arena, such as barrels, poles, and jump stands. He spent the next couple hours teaching them how to direct Roy through the different obstacles from the ground.

Marie was the only one who even got a chance to get in the saddle and it was only for a few brief moments. He had her mount, sit, back up a few steps, then dismount. He instructed her to do this three times, then said he was going to call it quits and headed out of the arena.

Ruth and Marie worked on putting the obstacle course away, letting Roy wander the arena as they did so. When they were finished, they removed Roy's tack in the barn and let him back out to pasture.

Ruth told Marie she could finish mucking out stalls, then seek out Ezra for further instructions on chores.

Marie nodded before heading off to finish mucking.

Ruth leaned against the tack room door for a minute, trying to catch her breath and cool down from the heat. After a few minutes, Ruth went back into the house and headed to her room.

Ruth peeled off her sweaty clothes and collapsed gratefully onto her bed. A knock sounded on her door. She groaned, rolled herself up in her sheets, and called, "Yes?"

Her father opened the door. "I need you to help Devin clear out the trails in the woods today."

Ruth groaned. "That's such hard work though!"

Her father smiled. "It's good for you."

Ruth sighed loudly. "Okay."

He nodded and closed her door.

She crawled out of bed to put new clothes on so she didn't feel quite as sticky. She was not looking forward to the work ahead of her, her body was already aching from the day's activities. At least there were only a few hours left before Devin and Ezra would be going home, then she could relax. She hoped so at least.

~ Chapter 7: Over The Phone ~

The next morning Ruth woke up and rolled her aching body out of bed. She checked her phone and saw a missed call from Charlene the previous evening. Strange, she usually had to be the one to contact her friends from Wisconsin.

She went to bed early last night, and while she didn't feel tired, she hurt all over. Too much work. It couldn't be nearly as good for her health as her dad and granddad made it sound.

Her father wasn't at the breakfast table, but Sophia informed her that he wanted her to work on clearing out the trails again; her heart sank. It did, however, make her feel better to know they were making progress. The trails close to the house had already been cleaned and they were branching out. She just hoped her father wouldn't get the idea to make new trails.

Ruth told Ezra to help Marie when she arrived and then went to find Devin. He was getting the ATVs ready to work on the trails. "You ready?" she asked.

"Almost," he smiled, his teeth bright against his dark

lips.

A few minutes later they were on the trails and working hard. They didn't talk much, Ruth feeling too exhausted to put forth the effort.

After several hours, Ruth's phone started vibrating. It was Sophia according to her caller ID, but they were so far out in the woods she only had one bar of reception. She answered but Sophia's voice was crackling so, she couldn't understand.

"What?!" Ruth yelled into the phone.

All she heard were garbles, then the call was dropped.

Ruth looked toward Devin, he was standing and fixed his eyes on her with a questioning look.

"I think that it's time for lunch because that was Sophia. We probably just can't hear the dinner triangle out here."

"Ah." Devin nodded.

They finished loading up the piles of branches they had, then headed back. Sophia called once more but the call was disconnected. They made it back to the barn and decided to unload after lunch.

The first thing Ruth did as she sat down was gulp down a glass of water.

Sophia raised an eyebrow in disapproval but didn't say a word.

Ruth glanced at her father and set her glass down when he cleared his throat. Everyone went silent as he prayed.

After consuming her first plate of food and serving herself a second helping, Ruth spoke up, "Dad?"

"Yes, hon'?"

"Can I be done for the day? I'm exhausted."

"Marie is supposed to be coming this afternoon."

"Ezra said she could help her."

"So, you're just going to be a lazy bones?"

"I suppose so."

"Well, that's fine, I guess. You just won't get paid for the time you don't work."

"Yes, I know that, I'm just so tired! I feel like my bones are too large for my muscles and tendons. My muscles shake when I pick stuff up."

Devin sniggered.

Ruth cast a glance at him, an eyebrow raised in defiance.

"Devin," Peter said, pointing a fork in his direction, "has been working like this for weeks, full days at a time."

"Well, I'm weak, what can I say?"

Grandpa Malachi chortled. "Well, there's somethin'

we can all agree to."

"Amen tah that!" Sophia spoke up.

Everyone started chuckling and laughing.

"Go ahead, laugh it up! I will remember this time of treachery!" Ruth shot back. That just caused everyone to laugh harder. Ruth rolled her eyes and laughed in a ridiculous, mocking manner, "Tee hee hee."

After a few minutes, everyone quieted and went back to eating. Ruth knew it was all in good fun and her mind soon wandered back to Wisconsin. She loved Missouri; it was beautiful. She could take or leave most of the people, but the horses were fantastic. Yet she missed Wisconsin, it was what she had always known. She decided to call Charlene after she got done eating.

The rest of lunch was filled with idle chatter, except a few quips between Sophia and Malachi, who would share smiles and coy glances while talking. When she was finished, Ruth put her dishes in the sink in the kitchen, then headed up to her room.

Ruth plopped onto her bed, pulled her phone out, and dialed Charlene.

To her surprise, her best friend in Wisconsin answered. "How's it going?!" she asked from the other end.

"It's going." Ruth wasn't sure how else to respond. It was good and bad at the same time.

"How are the horses?"

"Awesome!" Ruth said honestly. "What about yours?"

"Good, good. The ranch I board at just got a miniature horse, it's so adorable!"

"Aw!"

"Do you have any miniatures at your place?"

"No, we just have normal sized horses," Ruth paused, "and a Clydesdale."

"Aw, it would be so cute if we could get them together somehow! The little mini and the Clydesdale!"

Ruth chuckled. "I bet it would be an adorable picture."

"I miss you so much!"

"I miss you guys, too!"

"What are the people like down there?"

"Oh, just crazy."

Charlene laughed. "I bet. Are they hicks? Say crazy southern things?"

"Some of them, but hey, people are crazy everywhere. I mean, in Wisconsin people say crazy northern things and there are definitely some rednecks up there."

"Yeah, like what crazy things?"

"I'm sure you've heard some." She giggled as she told her friend, "Down here they think it's crazy to say, 'eh.'"

"Really?"

"Yeah, they think that only Canadians use that word."

Charlene chuckled. "Do they say ya'll?"

"Sometimes. Not a lot. It really depends on the person. You have all types around here."

"Sophisticated types?"

"Well, there are some people that drive down from St. Louis to vacation in this area."

"And do what?"

"Enjoy nature I guess."

"You guys should build cabins and rent them out."

"Not sure my dad would be up to that. This is sort of a hobby for him to begin with, you know, it's not his normal job."

"But he's got the money."

"Still..." Ruth paused and there was an awkward moment of silence, then she spoke up again. "So, what else is new besides the miniature horse at the barn? Do they still have the goat there?"

"You know they do!"

Ruth sighed as another awkward pause hung between them. "Wish we could see each other." Things were always less awkward when they were together in person. Talking over the phone made things difficult.

"You should come visit!"

The comment made Ruth think of the last time she drove to Wisconsin with her brother, David. No one took the time out of their day to see her. It struck a chord of resentment in her, but she couldn't be too mad, they were her best friends for years. Maybe they thought she wouldn't be a part of their lives anymore because she was so far away, and they were kind of writing her off. Maybe, she certainly hoped not.

"You could trailer your favorite horse up here and we could go riding together!"

Ruth chuckled. "That would be a lot of effort, I think I'd have to convince my father to buy the trailer, then drive it up there himself. I'm not sure he's willing to take that much time away from his work right now, he's already behind from moving."

"But he works over the internet!"

"Yeah, but he still works."

"I know." Charlene sighed.

Another awkward pause.

"Well, I have to go, my mother is taking me and my sisters out for girls' night!"

Ruth sighed softly. "Okay, talk to you later."

"Yep, catch you later." Charlene hung up.

Ruth fell back on her bed and closed her eyes. It was hard trying to have a friendship over the phone. Her life was changing and there wasn't much she could do about it. She opened her eyes and stared at the ceiling fan. She'd just have to try to hold on.

It was like riding a horse, she needed to learn from falling off and adjust her attitude before getting back on. If she could learn how to do that after getting banged up from falling off horses, she could learn how to push through life. One day at a time. No, more like one small step at a time. But for now, she was going to take a nap.

~ Chapter 8: Tim ~

Ruth woke the next morning determined to feel better about life than the day before. Overall, she couldn't complain too much. Life was pretty good. She didn't have a mother but she had a father and brother, she had family. She lived on a beautiful ranch with amazing horses. She had already made friends with Ezra and Marie even though it was still summer and school hadn't started.

School. Ugh. She didn't even want to think about it. She still had some time. Maybe it wouldn't be as bad as she thought. Maybe she could be homeschooled? She knew what the answer to that would be without asking her father. He'd make her go to school, probably after giving a speech about how it builds character.

Oh well, she'd make it through. If other people could do it, she could, too. Besides, she might find she liked it and Marie should be there, which would make it easier. She had a pretty good life. She also had Christ as a friend and counselor. He gave her strength day to day, and helped keep her from getting trampled by horses.

Ruth made it to the barn and decided to visit

Butterscotch, the neglected mare that was under recovery. She was doing a lot better and even whinnied when Ruth went up to her stall. She poked her nose over the stall door and sniffed at Ruth. Ruth held her hand out and Butterscotch nuzzled it.

Reaching up, Ruth scratched the mare under her right ear, between her jaw and neck. The mare nodded her head up and down slightly, showing her enjoyment.

"Hey."

Hearing the voice behind her, Ruth spun around and saw Ezra across the aisle, halter in hand, she must be doing the morning feedings of the horses. Devin usually did that, but maybe he was working on the trails or something. "Hey," Ruth smiled at her.

"I was wonderin'," her voice started cracking and she cleared her throat. "I was wonderin' if ya meant what you said about talkin' tah my parents about... ya know."

Ruth gave her what she hoped was a supportive smile. "Of course I did."

"Okay, that would be great." She coughed, glancing down at the ground for a moment before meeting Ruth's gaze again.

Ruth wondered why Ezra didn't want Tim to tell her parents with her.

"I talked to Tim last night."

Ruth braced herself. She had the feeling Ezra was about to answer her question about Tim.

"He…" she swallowed hard, "he dumped me."

Ruth stood in shock for a moment. *'What a slimbag.'* She realized that her jaw had literally fallen partway open in surprise and she shut it, hoping her shock wasn't making the situation harder for Ezra. "Of course I'll go with you to tell your parents. Have you told anyone other than me or Tim?"

Ezra shook her head, clearly fighting back tears.

Ruth paused for a moment. "When do you went to tell your parents?"

Ezra shrugged, a frown on her face.

Ruth swallowed, feeling awkward and unsure. What could she say to make Ezra feel better? "Well just let me know when you want to tell them, I'm available whenever you need me."

Ezra nodded, her eyes locking with Ruth, as if she was trying to express gratitude with a look. She gave a hesitant smile then tilted her head down and hurried off down the aisle.

Ruth watched her go for a while then decided to get the grooming bucket and spend some time with Butterscotch. She moved into the mare's stall and looked at the cream-colored mare in thought. Maybe Ezra should be the one in the stall, grooming the mare. She needed the comfort more than Ruth did.

Her father would still need the work assigned to Ezra to get done, but what if she just traded her for her work? If her father asked, she could just tell him it was her idea and Ezra was going through a rough time right now.

'*Good plan,*' she thought to herself and set the grooming bucket outside the stall door before going to find Ezra.

She found Ezra rather quickly, scooping manure out of a stall.

"Hey, Ezra."

Ezra turned to look at her. "Yes?"

"How about we trade jobs for a while? Butterscotch needs a good brush down and I could use some money, so I'll do your job for a bit."

She smiled softly. "Okay, but when I'm done I'll have to come help out again. It's not like I can sit in the stall all day without risking my job."

"I know."

"Okay." She handed Ruth the manure fork as she walked past. "Thanks."

Ruth began mucking the stall, quickly wondering if she made the right decision. '*No,*' she scolded herself, '*you did make the right decision. Ezra needs time with horses a lot more than you.*'

Ruth worked at a medium pace, trying to spare her still somewhat weary muscles from too much rapid movement, but not wanting to go so slow that if her father came out she'd get in trouble.

As it turned out, her father did come out and check on the barn. "Where's Ezra?"

"She was grooming Butterscotch last I checked." He probably walked past her but perhaps she was sitting down in the stall and he didn't see.

"And you're mucking the stall?"

"Yeah, I traded places with her for a bit."

"Why?"

"She... um... is going through a bit of a rough time at the moment."

"What sort of rough time?"

Poop, she hadn't planned on him asking that. "Well... um... it's kind of personal."

"But you know?"

"Yeah, but I'm not supposed to tell."

"Mhm. Well, I need to go talk to her. Is it okay if I go talk to my own employees even though I can't know what's going on with them?" he teased.

Ruth shrugged, "They're your employees."

"Oh, is that right? Glad you remember now." The half-smile on his face told Ruth he wasn't really upset.

"Well, I'm going to go talk to Ezra. See you later, hon', love you."

Ruth nodded. "See you, Dad. Love you, too."

He gave her one last smile before departing.

Ruth watched him go, wondering how everything would turn out for Ezra. She sent a quick prayer up to God, asking Him to have His hand in things and to give Ezra comfort. Then she sighed and went back to work.

~ Chapter 9: Waiting ~

Later that day, Ruth was helping Ezra feed the horses when Victoria arrived.

"Excuse me," she huffed from behind Ruth.

Ruth finished tying Roy's lead rope before turning.

"I need Winter's Pearl to be moved intah a stall twenty-four hours a day."

"Okay, are you needing us to change her diet?"

"No, not at this time. I just need her ready fer competition."

"That sounds like fun, are you doing a dressage competition?"

"Yes, I have a competition comin' up in a few weeks. Qualifyin' for regionals."

"Wow, that's exciting! So, you want her kept in the stall?"

"That's what I said. And keep her food regimen the same. I am goin' tah ride her right now though."

Ruth nodded, "Okay. She has already been fed and is in the pasture right now."

"Well, go get her fer me."

Ruth raised an eyebrow at her. "I'm currently in the middle of feeding Roy."

"Ezra can do that," she waved an arm toward Ezra, who was leading Embera out of the arena where the horses were being fed.

Ruth sighed. *'Do I look like your butler?'* She grumbled under her breath then went to the tack room to fetch a halter and lead. Victoria was leaning against a wall, her arms crossed as she waited for Ruth to retrieve her horse.

Ruth walked into the pasture and whistled loudly. Mirage came running but Winter's Pearl stayed in the pasture, ignoring Ruth. Ruth sighed, it was easier to catch Winter's Pearl when it was feeding time but after she was fed, it was difficult to get the mare to care about people being in her presence.

She headed slowly toward the mare, wondering how long she'd be in the field chasing the white horse. Well, gray horse technically. When Ruth got within two yards of Winter's Pearl, the mare moved off slowly. She stopped until the mare started to graze again.

As she got closer to the mare again, the horse snorted and walked off. Ruth sighed and stopped. The mare grunted and began grazing. Ruth moved out in a wider arc and approached more slowly, the mare moved off again.

Ruth hmphed and stopped. "Fine," she grunted at the

mare and turned, her back toward the mare. She kept her ears peeled, worried the mare might charge her as she had before, but she didn't hear any pounding hooves. She didn't hear much of anything.

"What the heck are ya doin'?!" Victoria yelled from the gate.

Ruth looked toward Victoria but didn't say anything. She didn't want to startle Winter's Pearl, then again, maybe focusing on something else would get the mare curious? "Waiting for her!"

Ruth had no idea if her plan would work and the worst part was she had to attempt it in front of Victoria. That way if her plan failed, the whole barn could know what an idiot she was. Oh well, it was too hot outside to run around the pasture with the mare for the next half hour, or hour, or two hours, or three.

Ruth waited, and waited, and waited.

"I don't think she's comin' to you!" Victoria yelled. "Come on, I want tah ride!"

"You can come get her if you want!" Ruth hollered. "But I'm not chasing her around the field!"

"I don't have all day!"

"I just want to try this!"

"Can't you do it on your own time?!"

I'm not exactly on your time.' "It's going to take

longer for me to chase her around."

No response from Victoria.

So, Ruth continued to wait. And wait. And wait.

Victoria stomped off after a while, likely to find someone to complain to.

Ruth kept waiting, she didn't even know she could have so much patience.

Ruth heard hoofbeats behind her and tried not to tense up. They were slow and soft, she hoped they meant Winter's Pearl had changed her mind about being uninterested.

She felt a snort of air on the back of her neck and the top of her shoulder. Thrilled that her experiment work, she turned around to see Mirage standing and looking at her with a quizzical expression. Ruth sighed in frustration as she realized that Winter's Pearl hadn't moved from her original position. She pet the blue roan on the nose and then scratched gently between her ears.

She glanced over at Winter's pearl to find the Lipizzaner looking at them curiously. Ruth chuckled and continued to show Mirage affection. She ignored Winter's Pearl. Out of the corner of her eye she noticed the grey mare inching closer. After a few feet, the mare stopped and began grazing, apparently either no longer interested or wanting to no longer appear interested.

"Hey girl," Ruth said softly to Mirage, "thanks for coming over but it was actually Winter's Pearl I was trying to intrigue." She pet the mare for a few moments more, then once again turned around and sent a silent, somewhat frustrated prayer heavenward, hoping that all of her patience and effort would not be for naught.

She heard Mirage moving away, and then nothing except for the chirping of the birds.

"Oh, come on!" Ruth looked toward the pasture gate to see Victoria once more standing there in frustration.

"If *you* want to chase this mare around the pasture, be my guest!" Ruth hollered.

The other girl didn't answer. She was still by herself, she must not have found someone willing to empathize with her situation.

Ruth sighed in hopelessness as she heard a horse approach and once more felt warm breath being blown across her neck and shoulders. Turning, her heart skipped a beat as she saw a white muzzle and realized the horse that had come to investigate was, in fact, Winter's Pearl. "Hey girl."

Ruth reached her hands out slowly and began to rub the mare on the neck. As the horse seemed to accept her, she put a halter and lead on and started to walk toward Victoria.

Ruth let herself out of the gate and handed the lead to

Victoria.

"About time, " she huffed as she grabbed the lead.

"If my performance isn't satisfactory, feel free to find someone else to retrieve your horse from the pasture, or even to take the initiative to do it yourself."

"That obviously won't be necessary since she's going tah be stalled in the future," Victoria sneered before stomping away with Winter's Pearl in tow.

Ruth shrugged, "You win some, you lose some." She closed the gate and went to see how Ezra was progressing with feeding the horses.

~ Chapter 10: Ezra's Parents ~

Ezra made plans with Ruth to visit her parents that evening, and Ruth asked her father if it was okay if she could hang with Ezra.

Peter paused for a moment as he leaned back in his office chair and interlaced his fingers. "Well," his mind seemed to be processing the request, "I suppose. Just try to make other friends, too, okay? Like Marie. If I have to fire Ezra, I don't want it to be awkward for you."

"You don't have to fire awesome people," Ruth chirped before thanking her father and departing his office. She hoped Ezra's pregnancy wouldn't cause any issues, but she couldn't see why it would.

She went downstairs slowly, her mind preoccupied with her thoughts. She didn't have many people to pick from when making friends. Maybe she'd make more when she went to school, but she couldn't be sure. Not many people seemed to like her. Maybe she was too blunt about things, or maybe too shy in groups. Whatever the case, making friends wasn't her strongest attribute.

If Ezra wanted to be her friend, she wasn't going to

walk on past. Sure, the girl made a mistake, but she seemed like a good person.

She hoped there wouldn't be any reason the friendship would put her father in an awkward place, but there were other jobs out there if need be. She ventured to the barn, so absorbed in her thoughts she tripped over Amerigo. She landed in the grass, palms out, and then rolled on to her back, laughing.

Amerigo sauntered up to her face, as if to check out his handiwork. His whiskers brushed her cheek as he meowed loudly. Ruth giggled, grabbing the ginger and white kitten, she pulled him against her side and pet him.

He squirmed away from her and she clutched at him, pulling him back. "No, stay here and be pet and like it. I need a friend."

Amerigo meowed in protest but ceased his squirming and laid down beside her. A few moments later she heard loud, irregular purrs rising from him.

"Hey, you ready?" Ezra's face followed her soft words, poking up above Ruth's face.

Ruth gave Amerigo a final rub on the head and then scrambled to her feet. "Yeah, just let me get my purse."

"Okay." Ezra trailed after Ruth but waited at the front porch while Ruth went inside the house.

"Alright, let's go!" Ruth said as she rejoined Ezra.

Ezra nodded and began to turn, but before she could rotate all the way, Ruth reached out and pulled her into a firm hug.

Ezra returned the hug tightly, a loud breath escaping her along with a shudder of anxiety. "Thank you," she said quietly.

"Of course," Ruth whispered before releasing the hug and the two walked quickly to Ezra's car.

They were both silent on the drive to Ezra's, and Ruth followed Ezra quietly to her front steps before Ezra stopped and turned to Ruth. "I'm not really sure how I'm goin' tah tell my parents. I've thought about it fifty different ways, but nothin' seems right. Thank you for coming with me, I really appreciate it."

"Of course," Ruth said, attempting a soft, supportive smile.

"Okay," Ezra took a deep breath and set her shoulders back before leading the way into her house. "Mom? Dad?" she called out.

"We're in the living room, honey!" a male voice responded.

Ezra swiftly flashed Ruth a half-smile before leading her into the living room.

Her mother and father were sitting on the couch with magazines spread across the coffee table in front of them.

The blonde hair atop Ezra's mother's head blazed as bright
as Ezra's, though her eyes were a different shade of blue.
Her father's hair, on the other hand, had a darker blonde
sheen and his eyes gleamed a soft brown.

"Hey, this is Ruth," Ezra motioned to Ruth as she
introduced her to her parents.

"It's a pleasure to meet you." Ruth smiled at them
and extended her hand to Ezra's mother first. After a quick
shake, she shook her father's hand.

"You as well," they both said in turn as they stood up
and briefly grasped her hand.

"So, you are Peter's daughter, right?" Ezra's mother
asked then motioned to a chair, "Why don't ya have a seat?"

"Thank you," Ruth said and made herself
comfortable in one of the chairs despite her pounding,
nervous heart. She cast a glance at Ezra, the poor girl must
be freaking. Ruth felt uncomfortable and she wasn't even the
one in the situation. "Yes, I am Peter's daughter," she
answered the question directed at her.

"Well, it was nice of your father tah give Ezra a job, I
know not everyone would be willin' tah take a chance on a
girl stable hand," Ezra's father offered.

"Yeah, that's how he is, he said she had all the
qualifications. She does a really great job." Ruth glanced at
Ezra to find her blushing. Must be a little awkward for the

girl, being talked about in the third person as if she wasn't there. Oh well, hopefully it was better than having to talk about the actual issue at hand. Ruth was beginning to understand the cliché about an elephant in the room and wondered if Ezra's parents could feel it as well.

"Well, that's good to hear," Ezra's father responded.

"Why don't you two go hang out, and we'll call ya when dinner's ready?" Ezra's mother said.

"Okay," Ruth agreed, looking toward Ezra.

Ezra nodded, jumping up from the chair she had found to sit in. "Okay, mom."

Ruth followed Ezra out, willing herself not to sprint out of the room before the elephant smooshed her.

Ezra lead Ruth to her room and then sat on the floor.

Ruth joined her and they glanced at each other before both looking awkwardly around the room and at the ground. "So…" Ruth said quietly.

Ezra let out a nervous giggle. "It's worse knowin' it's coming soon."

"Maybe it's not yours?" Ruth offered.

Ezra giggled in response. "Yeah, I wish."

"Well, it is what it is, we're just going to have to push through it."

"You don't have tah push through it, you're a really good friend for doin' this."

Ruth smiled at Ezra and wondered why she didn't have a best friend that would do it with her instead of asking Ruth. Really, they'd only known each other for a few months, it was kind of odd she had told her. Though she was curious, she decided it was best not to ask. If there was some sort of bad blood in relation to that, she didn't want to make matters worse by bringing it up. "So, have you decided on how you are going to break the news, or are you just going to say it when the opportunity comes up and hope it comes out the best way it can?"

"I guess the latter. Nothin' I have rehearsed in my head sounds right, but I don't think somethin' like this can ever sound right."

Ruth gave Ezra a sympathetic smile. "I suppose I can understand that."

The rest of the time in Ezra's room was rather uneventful. They made awkward, punctuated small talk until Ezra's mother called to them that dinner was ready.

~ Chapter 11: Unnecessary ~

Things were fairly quiet through dinner besides a few questions from Ezra's parents, mostly directed at Ruth. She answered them as best she could, they seemed nice enough at least. She glanced at Ezra occasionally throughout the dinner, it seemed the other girl was even more uncomfortable in her own home than Ruth was.

Ruth found herself getting second helpings of food in an attempt to make the dinner last longer, hoping to put off the conversation about Ezra's pregnancy. She almost asked for thirds when she realized it might be considered rude or piggish to eat that much, so she stopped herself. Then again, maybe they'd be complimented by her desire to eat so much of the food? She decided it was best not to risk it.

"The food was lovely, Mrs. Simon," Ruth said as she set her napkin down next to her plate. "Thank you."

"Of course, dear. It was nice tah meet ya."

Ezra's father started to stand and Ezra spoke up, "Dad, wait."

He looked at her curiously as he sat back down.

"I have somethin' tah tell you." Ezra took a deep

breath and stood up.

Ruth reached over to give her hand a gentle squeeze before returning it to her own lap.

By now, the eyes of Ezra's parents were widened in concern and confusion. Ruth could imagine some of the things that might be going through their heads.

"Well, ya both know Tim," Ezra began quietly.

Ruth noticed Ezra's father visibly tense at the mention of Ezra's now ex-boyfriend.

"Well…" she paused and then seemed to think it would be best to just say it, "I'm pregnant."

The silence in the room for the next several seconds was deafening.

Ezra's mother stared at Ruth, confusion plain across her wrinkled brow.

Ruth felt she should say something to break the silence but she was at a loss of what she could say. She just met the parents and really didn't even know Ezra that well. She'd never felt so out of place. She'd miscalculated how awkward the situation would be for her.

"Okay," Ezra's father said softly, seeming at a loss for words as well.

Ezra sat down slowly and glanced at Ruth.

Ruth gave her an encouraging smile. Why was she here again? She never felt more useless. "I hope I'm not imposing. I'm just here for moral support."

The look on the countenance of Ezra's mother turned thoughtful and she said, "That's sweet of you, but it's really not necessary."

"It's not like Ezra isn't our daughter because she made a mistake. She's having a child, okay, we'll figure it out," her father said quietly.

Holy cow, her parents were extremely understanding. Ezra really had nothing to be afraid of, even if she was a pregnant, unmarried teenager.

Ruth looked at Ezra, she felt she should leave but she was here for the other girl and wanted to make sure it was what Ezra wanted. Not that she could really go anywhere, she didn't have a car, but she could make herself scarce for a bit.

Ezra was staring at her parents, her mouth agape. Apparently, she had expected a different reaction from her parents.

"We'll always love ya, honey," Ezra's mother said softly.

"I love you both as well," Ezra responded. "Thank you."

Ruth pushed back from the table slightly and tried to make herself smaller so maybe they wouldn't notice the intrusion, but Ezra reached out under the table and grabbed her wrist. She must want her to stay, okay, then she would. Ruth reached her other hand over and placed it atop Ezra's to give it a gentle squeeze, letting her know she was there for her.

"How far along are you?" Mrs. Simon asked her daughter.

"About eight weeks."

Ezra's father cleared his throat and let out a deep sigh but didn't say anything. Ruth looked over at him and saw pain and conflict raging in his eyes.

"I know you guys don't know me very well," Ruth said quietly, hoping she was easing the tension and not increasing it, "but if you need anything, I'm happy to help."

"I noticed that," Mrs. Simon said. "I'm surprised you were willin' tah help Ezra with this, it was kind of you."

"Kind but unnecessary," her father grunted.

"Of course," her mother replied.

"I was scared," Ezra said hesitantly.

"We can understand that, honey, but there's nothing for ya to be afraid of," her mother said. "It will be hard, but we'll be there for you."

"Thank you."

Ruth shuffled her feet uncomfortably under the table. Could she leave now? She really wanted to go. She glanced toward where she knew the front door to be, then her attention returned to Ezra. She was here for her, this must be a lot harder for her, she would stay as long as she needed to, she resolved.

"It was really kind of you tah come," Ezra said softly.

"It was nothing," Ruth replied, *'compared to what you're going through,'* she added silently.

"I can drive ya home if you want," Mrs. Simon offered.

Ruth looked at Ezra, probably best, Ezra's face was wrinkled and her hands and shoulders were shaking slightly. She looked to be in no condition to drive. But did Ezra want her to go?

As if reading the question from her mind, Ezra glanced at Ruth and gave her a quick nod.

"Yes, Mrs. Simon, that would be very nice of you, thank you. Otherwise, I can call my Dad or brother?"

"It's okay, I'll take ya."

"Okay, thank you," Ruth said quietly. She waited for Ezra's mother to stand and back away from the table before following suit. She retrieved her purse and followed her to the car. They were mostly quiet during the drive, Ruth giving a few simple directions and pointing out turns.

As they turned into the driveway, Mrs. Simon spoke up, "Ruth?"

"Yes?"

"Thank you for comin' with Ezra. I could tell she's been wantin' tah tell us somethin', but I guess she didn't have the courage alone. It was good of ya tah come fer her."

"Of course."

"Does your father know?"

Ruth shook her head. "Just me and Tim as far as I know."

"That's why he left her?"

"Yeah," Ruth said quietly.

"Okay, dear," she reached over to squeeze Ruth's hand gently. "Have a good night."

Dear? Must be a southern thing, calling someone you just met "dear." "Thank you, you too." Ruth waited a moment before slowly getting out of the car and walking into the house. She tried to be quiet as she snuck up to her room, closed the door, and curled up on her bed.

Her intention was to go to sleep and escape from reality into dreams, but before sleep found her, she found herself crying. Hopefully Ezra would be okay, and the baby, too. The world could be a cruel place sometimes and she knew she hadn't seen the half of it.

~ Chapter 12: Encounter ~

Ruth half-expected Ezra not to show up to work the next day, but the teenage girl arrived early, as per the usual. She also wasn't expecting to see Victoria again so soon, but apparently the girl was serious about winning the dressage competition. She wasn't thrilled about seeing her, but that was life it seemed, she couldn't always pick and choose who did and didn't get to be part of her life.

Victoria suckered Devin into getting Winter's Pearl for her this time and Ruth was quite happy to have dodged that bullet. Ruth started the day by helping with chores, she didn't have much else to do anyway and it would be nice to have money, even if there weren't a lot of places for her to spend it out in the boonies as she was.

Yet, when Ruth walked past the outdoor arena where Victoria had had Devin help her set up a course and some woman was telling Victoria how to work with the horse, Ruth was intrigued. It was beautiful. Ruth had seen dressage on television a few times, but seeing it in person made it seem like a dance.

She stopped in her path and turned to watch.

Eventually she found herself drifting closer to the arena and she leaned against the arena railing. Victoria made a few minor mistakes that Ruth noticed, but overall, she was really good and had a great seat. Winter's Pearl, for being such a problem in the pasture, moved beautifully.

Ruth noticed despite the mare moving beautifully, she still fought Victoria. Her mouth was foaming slightly from pushing on the bit and there was a tie-down on her. It was obvious she knew what her rider wanted, but her head would toss slightly and her tail would swish in irritation.

Apparently, Ruth didn't know much about dressage though because Victoria's instructor was more than free with the criticism and she heard her grumble about "low-level horses." Ruth frowned at the comments and noticed Victoria was even more annoyed than usual when the lesson ended. She was yanking on Winter's Pearl's reins as she led the horse from the arena. She probably would have dragged the animal if it didn't weigh half a ton. Though part of Ruth wondered if Victoria might be capable of such a feat when she was in that grouchy of a mood.

Victoria's teacher turned to leave, her gaze falling on Ruth as she did so. Her eyes narrowed. "Can I help you?"

Ruth shook her head, "I was just passing by, I have some work to do."

"Watchin' the lessons fer free, huh?" The lady's

narrowed eyes were a clear indicator of her displeasure at the thought.

"I've just never seen dressage in real life before," Ruth replied, feeling a little awkward. It wasn't as if she couldn't go on YouTube and watch a hundred free dressage lesson videos if she had the notion. There were probably nicer people than that instructor doing the videos anyway. Watching people have lessons wasn't quite the same as getting them yourself. "Trust me, I had no intention of intruding." Ruth began to walk past the woman but was interrupted by her harsh tone.

"Young lady, what's your name?"

"Ruth."

"Ruth who? I just want tah talk tah the ranch owner."

Ruth narrowed her own eyes slightly and fought a smirk off her face. Was that supposed to be a threat? "Oh, you can just tell him his daughter, Ruth. He'll know who you mean."

Ruth only waited a moment before turning and leaving the woman standing by the arena, a slightly flabbergasted expression on her face. Part of her hoped the lady would talk to her dad and she could be there when it happened. Her father could be rather protective of his children.

Ruth decided making money could wait and headed

toward the house. She wanted to share the moment with someone, and while she liked the new girls, Marie and Ezra, she didn't know if they were really her friends. Not friends like those she had in Wisconsin, and Jill and Charlene immediately came to mind.

Ruth made it to her room without passing anyone and settled onto her bed, pulling out her phone. She dialed Jill first with no luck. She tried Charlene.

"Hello, girl!" came Charlene's voice from the other end.

"Hey, Charles!" Ruth replied.

"What's up?"

"Just calling to chat." Ruth wanted to tell Charlene what happened, but she decided to be polite and first ask, "What's new with you?"

"James is taking me on a date!"

Ruth almost gasped at the news. "What?! When did that happen?" *'Like really, I didn't even know he was interested in you like that. I thought you guys were just friends?'* Maybe her own interest in James had blinded her, but it was what it was now, she wasn't there, Charlene was. She could be happy for her friend.

"Last week! We're going out this Friday."

"What are you doing?"

"Going to dinner and a movie."

'*Cliché.*' "That sounds like fun! What movie?" It did sound like fun, even if Ruth was slightly jealous, she suddenly wanted a date. Stupid boys. She probably wouldn't get a date for years and years because she hardly even knew any guys and by the time she found one she wanted to date, she might be an old lady. She calmed herself with a deep breath, she was still a teenager, no need to worry. Yet. There'd be plenty of time for that later.

"I don't know yet. He said it's up to me, so I have to decide. Not sure if I should drag him to a chick flick or go to an action movie with him."

Ruth giggled. "What will happen after you're married? You know you like action movies, too."

Charlene gave a brief chuckle. "You're right, I do."

"So, go to an action movie with him."

"Okay, okay. You're so bossy."

"What about Drake?"

"I don't know, dating some girl named Janie I think? You know him, he doesn't really date, more like shows fleeting interest."

"Yes, I know Drake."

"And Jill?"

"I'm pretty sure she still thinks guys are designed to be punching bags."

Ruth chuckled. "Yeah, Jill can be kind of fierce."

"That's why we love her."

"One of the many reasons."

"Hey, I gotta go," Charlene said suddenly, a hyper note in her voice, as always. "Gotta see my horsie!"

Ruth chuckled softly, "Okay, Charles. Talk to you later."

"Bye!"

The line went dead.

Ruth hadn't told anyone about the moment with Victoria's teacher. Probably for the best she didn't gossip or gloat anyway. She sighed in frustration and fell back on her bed. Being alone sucked sometimes. At least she had her family, but she missed Wisconsin. She missed her friends.

Maybe going to school would actually be a distraction from her misery. Maybe it would be a welcome change. Imagine that. Her life really was going down the tubes to even have such a thought. Ruth stared up at the ceiling. She needed an activity to do. Something to get her mind off her friends and her hometown.

St. Louis with David. That would be a good place to have a little bit of fun and not have to think about missing her old home. She hopped out of bed and went to find her father to ask for the money she was owed for chores.

~ Chapter 13: Green-Eyed Boy ~

After getting off his serving shift, David agreed to take Ruth to St. Louis tomorrow, since he was off anyway. Finally, Ruth would get to be around civilization and have stuff to do again! The rest of the day went by rather quickly and the next morning, Ruth woke early to help take care of the horses before showering and dressing for the trip.

The first place they went was the zoo. It was actually pretty fun because of David's antics and snarky comments. Sometimes, Ruth wanted to pop her brother in the face, but other times he could keep her laughing at the most ridiculous things.

They browsed the gift shop for a while as they passed through. Ruth felt her money from chores burning a hole in her pocket so she bought a little horse trinket bracelet and a horse shirt. For a moment, Ruth wondered why she didn't stay home and hang out with horses if she was going to just buy stuff regarding them anyway. She shrugged it off, she was no recluse!

"What next?" she asked David.

"Well I suppose we should go to the Arch, only

makes sense."

"Sounds good to me."

The line for the Arch wasn't as bad as Ruth thought it would be and they got to the elevator in a matter of minutes. Ruth bumped into a teenage boy on her way into the small elevator opening and she blushed.

The boy was tall, he had to be around six feet. His cheeks flushed slightly as well and he backed up, dipping his head. "You first," he said softly, his emerald eyes locked on her.

She smiled bashfully and brushed past him. "Thanks."

He sat down next to his friend in the small elevator. Ruth noticed David intentionally left space so she would sit on the outside of the elevator where no one could sit next to her but him.

The ride up was pretty quiet except the creaking of the elevator and then everyone tumbled out, excited to head into the hallway at the top of the Arch. Ruth almost bumped into the teenage boy again but he stepped back, letting her pass once more. She couldn't hide the blush on her cheeks. Stupid hormones. *'Get control of yourself!'*

David conveniently positioned himself between Ruth and the boy.

The Arch was not quite what Ruth expected. She

wasn't sure what she expected, but as she stood at the top of the tower looking down, she knew that wasn't it.

Ruth glanced over and realized David must have gone to the other side of the Arch.

"Hey."

Ruth looked over her other shoulder to see the young man standing next to her.

"Beautiful, isn't it?"

"Yeah," Ruth said quietly.

"You from around here?"

Ruth shook her head. "Sainte Genevieve."

"No way, really? I'm from Farmington."

Ruth chuckled. "Wow, somewhere I actually know."

"I'm Troy, by the way." He extended his hand and Ruth shook it.

As if a sensor went off from Ruth making contact with a boy, David was there all of a sudden. "So, what do you think?" he said, wrapping an arm around her shoulders.

"Ruth," Ruth said quickly to Troy before turning her attention to her brother. "It's cool."

"Want to go somewhere for a bit? I'm starving."

"Yeah, me too. That sounds good."

He pulled her to the other side of the Arch, seemingly to get away from Troy. "Anywhere in particular you want to go?"

Ruth shook David off and shrugged, glancing back at Troy.

He was looking at her and he smiled softly before shifting to look back out the window.

Ruth smiled back quickly and then turned to her own window, shrugging as she remembered David was waiting for an answer. "I don't know, wherever."

"Okay, let's go."

They caught a ride down and David picked a pizza place. Typical. It was really good though.

Ruth tried to make conversation with David but her mind kept drifting to Troy. She'd probably never see him again, it was pointless to even think about him.

After eating, David asked what she'd like to do next and they decided to take a stroll by the river. Luckily, David was feeling rather talkative and he kept Ruth's mind off Troy for the most part.

The river was beautiful and Ruth had to admit she enjoyed the trip to St. Louis with her brother, even if he was somewhat overprotective. Not that her and Troy would have gone anywhere or done anything anyway. Though it was coincidental to meet someone in St. Louis from Farmington, maybe they'd meet again?

David turned the radio on during the car ride home, so the conversation was less stimulating and Ruth found her mind wandering again. The black-haired and green-eyed boy was foremost on her mind. She shook her head as his face entered her mind. Boys. What trouble.

She couldn't help but imagine what it might be like to run into him at a restaurant or store in Farmington though. How awesome would that be? She glanced over at David subconsciously, almost as if she was afraid he could read her mind. She shook her head. Even if he could, what could he say? Boys were going to be on her mind sometimes. Girls were bound to be on his mind sometimes. Probably most of the time. All of the time.

"I'm hungry again," David said suddenly, half-way home.

Well, girls were probably on his mind all of the time that food wasn't. "Okay, food sounds good to me."

He picked a fast food place. He pulled over in the parking lot to eat the food in the car. Why they didn't go in Ruth wasn't quite sure, but she wasn't going to complain.

David muttered something about his arm twitching before they prayed. Then they began eating and midway through munching down their meal, David punched his arm.

Startled, Ruth turned her head and raised her eyebrows at him. "What the heck?"

"My stupid arm won't stop twitching!"

Ruth looked at his arm, and sure enough, there was a

spot on his bicep twitching slightly. "I'm sure it will go away eventually, but you don't have to become violent."

He took his belt off and wrapped it around his muscle. He pulled on it, tightening it around his twitching muscle.

Ruth's eyes widened. "What the heck?! You're crazy." She shook her head, knowing her brother was a little crazy and she wouldn't be able to stop him.

He pulled the belt from his arm after a few drawn out seconds and his muscle had stopped twitching. Poor twitch, it was suffocated.

They finished the rest of the meal mostly silent, except for random chortles from Ruth whenever she thought about her crazy brother. She couldn't deny she loved him.

Overall, Ruth considered the trip a success though she was happy when they made it home and she could curl up on her bed to fall asleep.

~ Chapter 14: Future Plans ~

The next day, Ruth donned the new horse shirt and bracelet she bought and went out to greet the horses. Butterscotch was feeling lively for the morning because as Ruth walked into the barn she popped her head over the stall and whinnied. Must want her breakfast.

Ruth chuckled and said, "Just a minute girl, I'm working on it."

Ruth bumped into Ezra as she went to get feed. "Working on Butterscotch?"

"Yeah," Ezra said softly. Her eyes were warm and Ruth couldn't help but smile at her.

"Are you feeling better?"

"Feelin' morning sickness but other than that, not bad. My parents took the pregnancy well."

"You should have told me," came a deep voice from behind them. Ruth cringed as she immediately recognized it as her father's. What was he doing in the barn so early?

The two girls slowly turned.

A soft frown was on Peter's lips and his head was tilted downward slightly, one eyebrow raised. "It's not like

I'm going to fire you or something."

Ezra gulped loudly and Ruth glanced over to find her blushing. "I…"

"She's still really early."

Peter's eyes fell on Ruth. "And you didn't tell me either?"

"She asked me not to."

Ruth couldn't tell if the response in his eyes was pride or disappointment. His gaze fell back on Ezra. "Well let me know if you need anything." He walked up and grabbed a halter. "Have you fed Mirage?"

"No," Ezra said softly.

"Okay, well I'll take care of it." With that, he walked away, leaving Ruth and Ezra standing with confused expressions.

"Is he going for a ride?" Ruth asked.

"Probably, he does occasionally."

"I've never noticed."

"You're not the most observant," Ezra remarked.

"Well gee, thanks."

Ezra giggled then quietly said, "I can't believe he heard us talkin'…"

"I'm sure it will be fine."

"But he knows that I'm…"

"Yeah, it's not like he's going to tell anyone."

"But what about my job?"

"I'm sure it's secure," Ruth assured her.

Ezra sighed and rubbed the back of her neck. "I suppose people were bound tah find out sooner or later."

"It will be fine I'm sure. You have more important things to worry about than your job."

A pained expression crossed Ezra's face, twisting it slightly in fear. "I'm just really glad my parents are willin' tah support me through it."

"Are you going to keep the baby?"

"I haven't decided. I mean, it's my baby but I don't know that I can give it the best home it could have. It could probably have a better life somewhere else," she paused with a frown, "or a worse life. I just want to make sure he or she gets the best chance possible despite the fact her parents made a mistake."

"I'm pretty sure there are Christian adoption agencies that you could put it into. That way someone who really wants a child and can't have one, could love her. Or him. I think sometimes you even get to meet the parents."

"I'm sure you are right. There are a lot of different adoption agencies out there. There has tah be a good one I can put the baby into," her voice faltered slightly. "If I give it up that is."

"I understand, it must be a hard decision."

"It's just, it's still my baby, ya know?"

"I know, but I thought that was why you were thinking of giving it up for adoption, because you care about it and want it to have the best life possible. A life you can't give it. Would your parents raise it?"

"Maybe... but I don't know that I should even ask them tah put themselves in that position. I mean, they aren't exactly plannin' on more kids. Besides, if I do end up givin' it up, there is probably a couple somewhere who really wants a child. I just..." she trailed off, her mouth hanging half open as she gave Ruth a bewildered look, seeming unable to continue.

"You have time to decide," Ruth assured her. Then, on impulse, she reached over and gave Ezra a tight hug.

A shudder ran through Ezra and a loud sigh escaped her as Ruth embraced her. Ezra's head leaned on the other girl's shoulder and neither of them said anything for several long moments.

Finally, Ruth broke the silence. "Do you want to go for a ride?"

"Um... I have tah finish feedin' the horses," Ezra said as she pulled back from Ruth. "And, uh, I have tah pick up some more feed from the store and stack it in the feed room, or hay loft, accordingly."

"Aren't you supposed to exercise the horses?"

"Well, yes, occasionally, if they aren't gettin' enough attention, but I..."

"Look," Ruth said, twisting her hands together slightly. She hated that she was making the other girl uncomfortable. She only wanted to go for a ride. She lived on a horse ranch for crying out loud, was that too much to ask? But Ezra was right, her assigned chores had to be completed first. It just would be nice to have a riding partner. Even if they rode in silence there was just something about taking a horse out on a trail ride with someone else. It was peaceful and made the world somehow feel whole and right. "I don't want to get in the way of your chores or anything. I'm not trying to push you into anything."

Ezra's cheeks flushed in response and she was quick to say, "Well, no! It's not that at all. I'd love tah go ridin' with ya, I just have tah finish some things that your father told me-"

Ruth cut her off, feeling extremely out of place. "I didn't mean that. I mean, I wasn't trying to say that you are trying to avoid me or anything. I just mean, I wasn't trying to pressure you into avoiding your chores to hang out with me. I just thought that exercising the horses was part of your duties and I would really like to have a riding partner. But I wasn't trying to push you into neglecting anything that really needs done right now."

"Oh, I-I'm sorry, I misuh-understood," the normally composed Ezra was stumbling over her words somewhat and Ruth subconsciously took a step back from her, as if hoping it would make her appear less threatening.

"It's okay, Ez. Just let me know if you have free time later and we can go for a ride. My dad obviously took Jet out, but we could take Embera and Mirage, or Roy? I think I'm just going to, um, groom Butterscotch," Ruth said quickly, starting to back out of the feed room, grabbing a grooming bucket on the way.

"Embera and Roy might be the best choices. I think they would most benefit from bein' worked with."

Of course, always the sensible one. "Yes, of course, you're right." Ruth nodded her head at Ezra. "Well, see ya!" she said, heading out of the feed room before ducking into Butterscotch's stall.

~ Chapter 15: Learning to Teach ~

Ruth spent some time grooming Butterscotch, then decided to braid the mare's mane while she waited for Ezra. As she got down to the last few inches of hair she began to wonder if she should find something else to occupy her time. What if Ezra wasn't available until late afternoon? She might have time to braid the manes of all the horses before Ezra would be free. Ruth sighed and leaned her forehead against the cream-colored mare, her black hair falling about her face.

"Somethin' wrong, Ruthie?"

Ruth looked up as she heard her grandfather's voice. She knew it was him immediately because he was the only one that called her 'Ruthie.' She thought about teasing him by adding 'ie' to his name but it didn't work well when he was already Malachi. Malachi-ie seemed like it'd be more work to say than it was worth. Ah well.

"Hey, Grandpa." She offered him a soft smile. "Nothing. Just waiting for Ezra to free up some time so we can exercise the horses."

"Ah. Well if you would like I could use your help while ya wait. Though, I'm not sure how long we'll be, so

Ezra may end up havin' tah wait fer you."

"That's fine. I'll just text her, since I don't know where she is right now." Ruth did so and as she stood she wondered what Grandpa had in mind. Such blind faith in her family might leave her caught off guard. "Wait," Ruth paused, her hand on the stall door. "What exactly do you need my help with?"

Grandpa Malachi chuckled softly. "I was surprised ya didn't ask that question immediately. His grin was slightly mischievous as he answered, "Just goin' tah work with a problem horse. Thought ya might wanna come watch."

"I didn't know people hired you to help them with their horses?"

"Only occasionally. I have more time now that I'm retired. When people need the help, I'm happy tah help them. Well, happy tah help the horses mostly, and some of the people. I do what I can. They can't tell the people what the issue is, so I do my best tah listen to the language they can speak."

Ruth raised an eyebrow in confusion at her grandfather as she let herself out of the stall. "And what language is that? Mandarin?"

Malachi chuckled. "What do ya really think it is?"

"Horse?"

Malachi shook his head as the two of them walked

toward the driveway. "It's body language."

Ruth rolled her eyes. "Okay, Grandpa. I get it."

"Do you?"

"I get what you're saying. That doesn't mean I'm saying I can listen to it and read it well. Not like you, I'm sure."

He laughed softly. "Just takes learnin' and practice. Every horse is different but not as different as ya might think."

"Makes a lot of sense, Grandpa," Ruth said, her dry tone slightly sarcastic.

"Kind of like people."

Ruth smiled softly to herself. Was that really true? Because so far the people in Missouri seemed to be way different than those from Wisconsin. Were there similarities in everyone? If she went to a different country it would probably be an entirely different ball game.

As if sensing her thoughts, Grandpa added. "Yeah, people are people. A lot of the time trends that people want tah act are all new, really ain't that crazy and different if you look at history. People are individuals but we all have the same basic needs. And we are all in need of a savior."

He had her there.

The drive to the owner with the troublesome horse started out quiet but it seemed that wasn't good enough for

Grandpa. He wanted to get to know his granddaughter better or something because he broke the silence with, "Met any cute boys yet?"

"Where would I have met cute boys?"

"Horse shows?"

"I haven't been to any yet."

"What? Just in Missouri or ever?"

"I'm not even trained in an equine sport, and even if I was, where would I get a horse to ride that was trained in at as well?"

"Ruth," Grandpa said blandly, "ya live on a horse ranch."

"But none of those horses are show horses."

"Mirage is trained on barrels."

"Mirage is as old as you."

Grandpa laughed softly. "I'm glad ya think I'm so young."

Ruth glanced at him and when he looked over to meet her gaze, she noticed a sparkle of humor in his sapphire eyes.

"So, what about barrel racin'?" Malachi prodded after a few seconds.

"I don't know, it doesn't really seem like my thing."

"How so?"

"Seems the same over and over."

"Ya want somethin' freestyle, hm?"

"Yeah, like dressage or... or..."

"So, dressage."

Ruth laughed softly. "Yeah, I saw Victoria doing it with Winter's Pearl and I can't help but want to try it myself. It's like dancing with the horses."

"Ya could just dance with the horses as well."

"What? How do you mean? Does Mirage know the waltz as well as barrels?" she teased.

A laugh rumbled from Grandpa's chest. "Not quite, but she does know a few tricks. Maybe I can show ya sometime and you can begin tah learn them."

"That would be awesome!"

"I wanna warn you, though, that ya can't expect any horse to just pick these things up. You want a horse tah love and respect ya, you need to spend time with it. It's harder to dance when a horse doesn't want to be with you."

"Do they step on your feet or something?" Ruth snorted.

"No, ya get tangled up in the lines, or if ya do it without lines, they run off."

"You do this stuff freestyle?"

"Makes it simpler."

"And Mirage just follows you?"

He didn't answer, his lips pursed in a somewhat

amused affirmation.

"I've never had a horse want to be with me enough to follow me around off the halter and lead."

"Ever have a dog do that?"

"Yeah."

"A cat?"

"No."

He chuckled. "Fair enough. I have had a cat do that. Though that answer kind of wrecked where I was headed with my point."

"What is your point, Grandpa?"

"How do ya think that dog, whichever one you knew, would feel, if all ya did was grab it, cinch a saddle on, and ride around? Kick him tah go, yank on his mouth tah stop, and smack him if he didn't do what ya wanted?"

"I guess it depends on the dog, I suppose the majority of them would end up biting you."

"Be a lot less willin' tah follow ya around, no?"

"Well, yeah."

"Now imagine if that dog was two or three times your size. Would ya even dream of doin' those things tah that dog?"

"Heck no," Ruth responded readily. "I like my flesh attached to my body."

"Aye, me too. I think most people do."

"Yeah, I'd agree with that assessment."

"Yet they do those same things tah horses everyday."

"But most horses aren't as liable to bite..." Ruth trailed off, the moment with Winter's Pearl flashing in her mind once more. Which was worse, being bitten by a dog or trampled by hooves attached to a half-ton beast? She hoped she'd never find out. "Okay, I see your point, Grandpa. But what do you do then?"

"Do fer what?"

"To make horses want to be with you?"

"I'm not an expert, but I'd say spendin' time with them where you aren't smackin' 'em and forcin' 'em tah do stuff would be a good start." He paused for a moment, seeming to be caught up in his thoughts before he began again. "Ever seen a horse that runs tah the gate at feedin' time, and then runs away from the gate whenever a human approaches not durin' feedin' time?"

"Yeah."

"People like tah act as if horses are stupid, but they aren't, they are very intelligent creatures. They know when it's feedin' time and when it's time fer everything else."

"So how do you stop that horse from running away?"

"Stop doin' what you're doin'."

"Wow, thanks, you're so informative, Gramps."

"I try, I try."

"No, for real. What can I do?"

"Well, ya could start by tryin' tah get the horse for things other than work. Maybe pick one horse tah start with and focus on while ya learn. Then ya can help other horses as you progress?"

Ruth nodded slowly, even though from her peripheral vision she knew Grandpa wasn't looking at her. "Okay, which horse?"

"That's up tah you."

Jet? Embera? Maybe Roy would be good to start with since Grandpa had already trained him on several things? Or even Mirage. Probably the best, Mirage, but yet... gah! How to decide?!

Grandpa chuckled softly after a few moments, seeming to know that she was struggling to make up her mind. "Might be a good idea tah start with a horse that has some experience already, so ya don't end up with more than ya can handle."

"So, Mirage?"

"Probably the best choice, but Roy's not a bad choice either. But honestly, it's best tah do it with a horse ya enjoy bein' around, then it's less likely that you'll peter out halfway through learnin'."

"I enjoy being around all horses."

"Why yes, ya do seem to, but I'd assume there's a

horse you've formed an attachment with?"

"*All* of them?"

Grandpa sighed, seeming a tad exasperated with the answer. "Do ya want tah learn or not?"

"Embera," Ruth answered quickly, hoping she wouldn't annoy her grandfather out of teaching her before the lessons even started.

"So, ya pick one of the nervous, flighty, young horses? Well, at least I know you'll be a good listener as a student."

Ruth giggled softly at his sarcastic comment. "Sorry, Grandpa, but you asked which horse I felt connected to."

"And it's Embera?"

"Well, I like all of them. I enjoy spending time with Jet a lot, too. Mirage does make me more comfortable because she's well-trained, but she's getting older and I don't want to spend all my time working with her and building a relationship when I know she might not be around all that long."

"Wow, that's a depressin' thought. And yet, here ya are, with me."

"Oh man, Grandpa, I totally didn't mean it like that."

"Old things haven't lost their value, ya know."

Ruth felt the warmth of a blush creep onto her cheeks. "Yeah, I know, Grandpa. I didn't mean it like that,

I'm sorry."

"I know, Ruthie. It's fine, ye're quite forgiven."

Ruth let out a soft sigh. Maybe she should think things through better before speaking, but what she'd said was true. It'd be harder to lose Mirage if she spent all her time and energy into training with the mare. Not that that wouldn't happen with any horse she worked with.

"Just think about it. If ya really want tah work with Embera, that's fine, but I don't want ya switchin' horses halfway through. Once you commit, ye're gonna have tah be committed to that horse fer a while."

Ruth nodded in acceptance. "Okay, Grandpa."

Grandpa pulled into a drive and they both became quiet until Grandpa put the car in park in front of the square, dark green house. "Her name is Susan," he noted.

~ Chapter 16: War Captain ~

The middle-aged woman that answered the door had flowing auburn hair running past her shoulders and kind brown eyes. "Ah, hello Malachi," she greeted him. "And who might this be?" she asked as her eyes fell to Ruth.

"This is my granddaughter, Ruthie."

He *would* introduce her as 'Ruthie.' He would. "Hello," Ruth said, a hint of shyness quivering her voice, "it's a pleasure to meet you."

"Same here," Susan said, offering a hand to shake.

Ruth couldn't help but widen her eyes in surprise when the woman fully grasped her hand and gave her a firm handshake. It'd been the first strong handshake she could remember from a woman since she'd left Wisconsin. Ruth found herself smiling back at the woman's intoxicating smile before her attention was turned to grandpa Malachi as her hand was released.

"Come meet the horse I was tellin' ya about, hm?" Susan said before leading the way to the small pasture behind her house.

The horse standing in the pasture was a docile-looking brown and white paint.

"This is War Captain," Susan said, gesturing to the horse in the field.

"So, he's the one you were tellin' me about."

"Yep, just got him a few months ago fer my grandson. He's been a bit hard tah handle though. I mean, he's not mean-tempered in anyway, but he doesn't really do anything. I thought he'd be good fer Zachary since he's so laid back, but he might be a tad too laid back."

"Yeah, ya mentioned over the phone that he's lazy," Grandpa replied as he let himself into the pasture.

"Yeah, he doesn't want tah do anything but eat."

"Is he smart?" Grandpa asked as the three of them walked through the field.

"I can't tell, really. He's stubborn. I don't think he's stupid per se, but I haven't really been able tah train him on anything because he just refuses tah do it. I don't know if he *can't* learn it or if he just won't."

"And ya can't get him tah go faster than a trot?"

"And that's a barely, he'll manage it a few seconds and then go tah a walk. He also likes tah stop randomly, I guess when he decides he's done walkin' fer the moment. I tried pushing him tah trot longer and he started getting bucky, which made me nervous."

"Ah," Grandpa said, walking into the shed that had

been set up as housing for the gelding. The side of the shed he walked into had tack hanging up on the wall and he pulled down a halter and lead, then found a lunge whip.

Susan and Ruth hung back in the pasture while they waited for Malachi. Ruth looked over to War Captain, the equine was busy munching on the grass. He seemed disinterested in the humans that had invaded his living space. Yet, Ruth noticed one ear was cocked towards her and Susan, and one ear was pointed toward the shed.

As Grandpa began to approach the gelding, the horse raised his head halfway and looked at the man. Then he looked away. Grandpa stopped his approach and smiled over at Ruth and Susan. "Is he hard tah catch?"

"Not really," Susan responded. "For the most part he just lets ya walk up tah him. If ya have a treat, he might even come toward you. I've only had him move away once or twice."

Grandpa coughed suddenly and then nodded in response. "Okay, good." As the paint swung his head back toward Grandpa, both his ears now perked forward in interest, Malachi began to approach him again.

The horse let him draw near, keeping wary eyes on him but not moving away. Grandpa reached out a hand, which the paint sniffed, then he moved over to stroke the horse along the base of the neck and shoulder. After a few moments, he slipped the halter over the gelding's head and then he kept petting.

Ruth watched with interest, curious what her grandfather would do.

"Have ya done any ground work with him?"

"Just some of the basics," Susan responded.

"Such as?"

"Lungin', havin' him respond to pressure from my hand on his skin and from shakin' the lunge whip."

"And he gets it?"

"Yeah, but like with lungin', he just doesn't want tah go faster than a walk. If ya lunge him, you will see, he gets cranky if ya try tah make him pick up the pace.

Grandpa nodded, coughing again before rubbing the gelding all across his neck and body. "Just goin' tah get him used tah me first."

After War Captain began to relax, Malachi took the lunge whip and began rubbing it over the horse.

Ruth watched with interest. This part seemed so important in Grandpa's mind but soon the gelding looked as if he was about to fall asleep with boredom. His head was lowered, his eyes half-lidded as he let out a long snort of air. "If your goal is to make the lazy horse fall asleep, I think you're almost there, Grandpa," Ruth teased.

He looked over at her and rolled his eyes, causing a

chitter of laughter to escape Ruth.

She glanced over at Susan to see a smirk on the woman's face as she continued to watch the old man working with her horse. "I've seen him work miracles before."

"Oh yeah, where?"

"Your grandfather is a bit of a legend with horse people in these parts. A lot of people call him when they have troublesome horses."

"Do you two actually know each other then, or do you just know of him by word of mouth?"

"Oh, a bit of both. That's kind of how it works around here. Kind of how it works around most small towns I'm assumin'."

Ruth nodded and looked back toward her grandfather. After a few moments, she asked, "So, what are you going to do to fix the horse, Grandpa?"

"The horse doesn't need fixin', we need to learn how tah listen and work with him accordingly.   Just because he has a different personality than we prefer, or are used to, doesn't make him bad or mean he needs fixin'. We can't expect tah change the horses, so we need to change the way we work with them."

"Where did you learn all this, Grandpa?"

"From the horses."

"How's that?"

"I didn't have a trainer growin' up, but I spent many a day down at the horse stables, doin' chores for free ridin' time." Malachi began pushing on different areas of War Captain, getting the horse to move away from pressure. The gelding already seemed to know what was expected of him and seemed willing enough to comply, though the look on his face could best be described as sheer boredom.

"Durin' that time I got tah ride a lotta different horses and learn how tah work with 'em. Without anyone there to teach me," he paused in his sentence as he began to get the gelding to move away from the steady pressure of a flicking lunge whip, the whip never actually touching the horse, "I had tah listen to the horses and read their body language as best I could, in order tah work with them and progress with skills."

"I see," Ruth responded, before silently watching her grandfather work.

After several minutes of making sure that War Captain would respond to the lunge whip flicked at different areas of his body, Malachi sent the horse out on a circle and had him start moving around. Susan was right, the paint did not want to move faster than a walk, and he even kicked out in a small buck when Grandpa urged him into a trot.

After a bit, Malachi let the horse slow down and then

invited him back into him. The gelding was more than happy to join the human, sniffing at him curiously as if searching for treats, but he soon became disinterested and lowered his muzzle to the grass.

Grandpa moved to the horse and began to pet him, then slowly rubbed the lunge whip over different areas of his body, gently looping it over the horse. After several minutes, the horse wasn't the only one bored, but Ruth continued to watch. His methods might seem time-consuming and a tad boring to start with, but they got results, she knew that from Mirage and Roy. She could tease, but Grandpa knew horses and she could learn a lot from him.

Finally, Grandpa removed War Captain's halter and lead. The paint sniffed at Grandpa for a moment then went back to grazing. Malachi turned to Ruth and Susan and approached them slowly, another cough wracking his body as he moved toward them.

"So?" Susan asked hopefully. "Think you can help him?"

"This is a rather smart horse. The question is, do ya have the time and patience tah handle him? Do ya have the willingness to learn and sometimes be beaten? Do ya have the drive tah actually become partners with this animal? There's nothin' wrong with the horse, he just needs tah be handled appropriately. He needs tah be mentally stimulated."

"Yes, I am aware of yer methods, and that I will need tah spend time learnin' how to work with the horse. Most everyone who knows of you, knows that ya don't 'fix' horses, you 'fix' how people work with them."

Ruth gave a soft chuckle but Grandpa nodded. "Well then, I can help ya."

"So, what's the problem?" Susan asked as the three of them headed out of the pasture.

"The main one I believe, is that he's bored."

"Seriously?"

"Quite."

"I'll see ya in a few days then?"

"Sounds good tah me."

After they had reached the car, Grandpa shook Susan's hand and then the woman turned to Ruth for a handshake. "It was a pleasure tah meet ya."

"Likewise."

"Will ya be comin' back with your grandfather to work with War Captain?"

"I hope so."

"Good, I look forward tah seein' ya." Susan flashed a charming smile and nodded her head slightly before heading back toward her house.

Ruth scrambled into the car, excitement bubbling within her. She spent the drive back to the ranch daydreaming about all the skills she would learn from Grandpa, and the things she would be able to do with horses after taking lessons. Most of her daydreams involved Embera. She couldn't wait to learn more.

~ Chapter 17: Quality Time ~

The training started the next day, for both Ruth and Embera. Grandpa said he had no time to waste, considering his excessive age, he might be found unnecessary at any minute. Ruth's only response was to roll her eyes.

The first thing Grandpa taught Ruth was not to approach Embera without permission. This went pretty easy since Mirage quickly noticed the duo and trotted over to them, the rest of the herd, aside from Winter's Pearl, trailing in her wake. After Mirage nuzzled at Grandpa for several minutes and momentarily at Ruth, she lost interest and began to graze.

This left an opening for the other horses, including Embera, to investigate if there were any goodies. Ruth slipped the halter on the mare and they followed Grandpa out of the pasture. After obtaining a lunge whip and a longer lead, Malachi led them out to the round pen. He dropped the whip and lead in the middle of the pen and walked out, leaving Ruth standing with her back turned to a horse that seemed equally confused.

Embera nuzzled Ruth's shoulder, sniffing her

curiously.

Ruth stood in the middle of the pen and gave her grandfather what she hoped was a plain old questioning look.

He leaned against the rails of the round pen, resting his forehead against one of the panels and watched her, as if expecting her to know the next step.

Ruth continued to stare.

No answer was forthcoming from Grandpa Malachi.

Somewhat to Ruth's surprise, Embera was still curiously nudging her shoulder. "Okay Grandpa," Ruth asked in confusion, "what now?"

"I was wonderin' if you were going tah ask or just stand there starin' at me." Her grandfather chuckled softly deep in his throat but doing so brought on a fit of frightful coughs.

"You were coughing yesterday as well, Grandpa. Are you okay?"

Grandpa waved his hand dismissively at Ruth. "I've been through a lot in my days, Ruthie. A simple cold is not goin' tah kill me."

"But..." Ruth was about to say that he was old and he needed to be more concerned for his health, but she stopped herself. Health reports were always saying that the elderly had weakened immune systems, but Malachi was sure to know such information and he was also sure not to be pleased at the brazenness of her pointing out his age to him. Again.

"But what? Would a little cold render you useless?"

"Well I would hope not, but..." she almost mentioned his age again. "Horse training can wait," she offered.

Another cough wracked Grandpa's form before he shook his head, straightened his shoulders and said, "Just focus on the horse, Ruthie."

Ruth frowned at him but decided to listen, figuring she didn't have much of a choice anyway. She couldn't force Malachi to take care of himself. Maybe if things continued to get worse she'd tell her father and see if he could help in some way.

After fending off another coughing fit, Grandpa instructed Ruth to rub the lunge whip over the mare's body as she had seen him do yesterday with War Captain.

She complied, moving slowly and trying to keep her body at ease as the mare's nostrils flared at the feel of the whip, her head raising in alarm. Ruth continued moving with slow, gentle movements, waiting patiently for the mare to relax before moving around the mare. She did her best to ignore the coughing coming from her grandfather outside the round pen even though each one sent a small shiver of fear coursing through her.

Ruth tried to keep her focus on the mare, and as

Embera began to relax, her head lowering, one ear twitching toward Ruth, she stopped her actions and looked over at her grandfather.

He was leaning against the round pen, and Ruth couldn't be sure but she thought he was shaking slightly. His head was tilted downward and she waited patiently for him to look back up at her. "Good job, Ruthie," he encouraged. He paused for another cough and then said, "Okay, now just let her go and hang out fer a bit."

"What?"

"If this was a dog or a cat, would ya not spend some time just hangin' out, givin' it attention when it was curious? Pettin' it, givin' it affection?"

'Even if I have to force it,' Ruth thought, remembering how she'd captured the protesting Amerigo the other day and forced him to be pet. "How long?"

"I don't know. Fifteen or twenty minutes at least."

"Can I read or something at least, while I hang out?"

The shrug of his shoulders seemed to indicate that Malachi was sighing, but the action brought on another bout of coughs. "If ya think ya must," he finally responded as the coughing ceased. "But I think I'm goin' tah go home and get some rest. I might be strong as an ox, but this is a killer cold."

Ruth watched him go with apprehension, wishing

there was something she could do. Her fingers tangled into Embera's mane and she leaned her forehead against the mare's neck, nervously whispering a prayer.

As if the mare could somehow understand what was going on, her head nodded slightly as Ruth quietly pleaded with God for her grandfather's health. After she had finished, Ruth removed the halter from the mare's head and slipped out of the round pen to find herself a book. She had debated bringing her laptop in the round pen, but decided it was too valuable to risk it getting crushed by a hoof.

Ruth found a book that looked somewhat interesting in the library, and pulled it half-heartedly from the shelf. Maybe one day she would like reading, maybe. She was her father's daughter, but they couldn't be alike in all things. So many books were boring compared to all the things she could be doing in real life.

Before heading back to the round pen, Ruth found a bucket she could sit on while she read. It was comfortable at first, but the book turned out to be rather interesting, and after a while Ruth noticed that the hard plastic was becoming less inviting by the moment. She realized she had forgotten about the horse in the round pen with her and looked up to find Embera standing about a yard away, her head raised halfway, she was looking at Ruth with curiosity, her ears perked forward.

"Hey girl," Ruth said softly. The mare's head raised higher at the sound of Ruth's voice as she snorted softly. "Not sure what to think of all this, are you?"

The mare approached with cautious steps, leaning her head out to sniff at Ruth as she got closer.

"Yeah, it's all a bit mysterious to me as well. I guess we're just supposed to get to know each other? Staring contest?"

The mare snorted softly and Ruth laughed quietly. Her eyes remained on the mare as hesitantly, the equine's muzzle came forward and pushed against Ruth's arm. Ruth reached out to stroke the horse's face gently, a soft smile playing on her lips. "We're going to get along fine, I think," she said quietly.

After a few minutes passed, Ruth stood. She set her book on the pail, retrieved the halter she had used earlier, and slipped it back over the chestnut's head. She led the mare out of the round pen, and released her back into the pasture just as the late morning sun decided to really make its presence known with rays of scorching heat.

Ruth put the bucket away and clutched her book against her as she retreated into the house, eager to seek shelter in the air conditioning before the sun decided to become unbearable.

~ Chapter 18: Plans ~

By the time Ruth heard the lunch triangle being rung by Sophia, her tummy was growling in hunger. It was almost as if it could hear the triangle and knew what it meant.

She stood up quickly, dropping the book on her nightstand. She headed out of her bedroom and down the stairs, where she was passed by David, and made it into the kitchen within moments. David, however, was already seated at the table by the time she got there, a grin plastered on his face.

She rolled her eyes as she took her place at the table, noticing there was no place set for Grandpa. Hopefully that meant he was getting some rest so he could recover from that troubling cold.

Soon enough Devin, Ezra, and Ruth's father ventured into the kitchen and took their places at the table as Sophia set the food out. Sophia took her place last and edged her chair close to the table. That's when Ruth noticed the worry lines on the woman's face and the frown upon her lips. Was she worried about Grandpa?

"Let's bow our heads for prayer," Ruth's father said

and she glanced over to him before complying.

Her father's prayer was brief but earnest. He prayed for blessing over the food and thanked the Lord for his family. Then he prayed for Grandpa, that he would get better soon and the Lord would heal him.

As her father ended the prayer, Ruth uttered a quick, "Amen," then glanced around the table. Her father, Sophia, and David all seemed varying degrees of concerned. Ezra and Devin, on the other hand, seemed a tad hesitant and confused.

As everyone began serving themselves up, Devin ventured to ask, "So, what uh, what's goin' on with Malachi?"

It was silent for several moments before Peter answered, "He's sick." There was a long pause, awkwardness filling the room before Peter continued. "He seems to have an awful cold and he went home to rest. A cold may not sound that serious but with him, if it's bad enough for him to take time to rest, it's pretty bad."

There was silence then. The truth of the words that Peter had just spoken looming ominously in the air. Hopefully he'd be better soon with the rest. Maybe by tomorrow he would be back on his feet, telling the world how things were. They could hope.

The rest of the meal was eaten in relative silence and

after Ezra had gotten up from the table, Ruth followed her outside.

"Hey," she said quietly.

Ezra turned around, one eyebrow cocked in question.

"Care to go for a ride?"

"Ya know, I've been thinkin', maybe it's not such a good idea for me tah ride right now."

"Why not?" Ruth asked before her eyes fell subconsciously to the girl's stomach. "Oh."

"I'd love to another time. After the baby comes. I'm just, I'm a little worried. Paranoid. I don't want tah do anything that might hurt it."

"Right." It struck Ruth as a tad ironic that something Ezra didn't want could so quickly turn into something she protected.

"Sorry, Ruth."

"No problem, um..." Ruth grappled for words, suddenly feeling self-conscious. "Maybe we can do something else tonight or something?" She felt like a little kid at the playground, begging, *'Please, I need a friend! Will you be my friend?'*

"Oh, oh yeah, sure!" Ezra responded, seeming slightly taken off guard by the comment but willing enough to agree. "What um, what would ya like tah do?" she added.

"Run around like a bunch of hooligans and cause

trouble?"

Ezra's eyes widened but she must have sensed it was a joke because a soft chuckle escaped her. "Maybe somethin' more suited fer Christian teenagers?"

'Like getting pregnant?' Ruth bit back, knowing the words would be more hurtful than humorous. "Such as?"

"I don't know, watchin' a movie?"

Fairly safe choice for people just getting to know each other. "Okay, sounds good. What sort of movie?"

"I don't know, we've got quite a few at my place. Maybe a romance?"

'Ugh, gag me,' Ruth responded in her mind. "Maybe we could just decide when we get to your place?"

"Okay, that sounds like a good idea tah me," Ezra agreed.

"So, is it on for tonight or just sometime?"

Ezra shrugged, a soft blush on her cheeks. "I... I don't know. What do you think?"

"I mean, I'm probably good for tonight if you are."

"Let me call my parents and get back tah ya later today?"

That sounded like a great idea since the sun was continuing to intensify in bearing down its waves of heat upon the earth. "Yeah, sounds good," Ruth agreed.

"Okay," Ezra said before offering a small smile and

turning to head toward the barn.

Ruth smiled as well and then headed toward the house, making her way back to her bedroom to once more curl up with the book she was reading, in the safety of the air conditioning.

~ Chapter 19: Just Here To Help ~

The verdict ended up being to Ruth's liking. Ezra's parents were fine with Ruth coming over and her own father was as well, though he seemed a tad distracted with his work when she asked.

As Ruth was drying off from her shower though, she suddenly felt a twinge of awkwardness in her gut. The one time she had met Ezra's parents was to help Ezra tell them she was pregnant. She probably wasn't their favorite person in the world. Oh well, she'd likely end up facing them sooner or later, and it wasn't as if she had anything to do with Ezra getting pregnant. She couldn't shake the sliver of anxiety in her gut as she picked out an outfit, though.

After she had finished getting dressed, Ruth realized there was still about twenty minutes left before Ezra was done with work. She made her way into the living room to play a game or two on the gaming console as she waited. David was already there, resting on the couch and driving a tank in some war game.

Ruth plopped ungracefully down next to him. "So, that looks boring." She'd never been good at driving things on games, she was better at shooting or exploring.

"That's simply because you are boring. The game is fun," David grunted.

"Aren't you supposed to be at work?" Ruth chimed. "Did you get fired already?"

"Servers have erratic schedules a lot. And we tend to trade our shifts."

"I doubt all of them do."

"Well, the servers where I work do, and today I am not scheduled, therefore I'm not at work."

"Ah, so instead of firing you, they just quit putting you on the schedule? Makes sense I guess, then they don't have to deal with the little hissy fit you're likely to throw if they told you you're fired."

David snorted an ironic half-laugh. "You-" whatever he was going to say was cut off by an enemy tank nailing his with a loud 'boom.' "Dang..." he muttered, veering off to the side but he was unable to avoid the following shots from the enemy, and his tank exploded in a colorful array of orange and red fire with billowing smoke.

"Well, you're right, that *was* kind of entertaining."

David dropped the controller and rolled his eyes at Ruth. "Some sister, celebrating when I get blown up."

"You didn't get blown up," Ruth sighed melodramatically. "A tank you were driving on a game got blown up. You are just fine, except maybe a touch of a black mark on your ego."

"My ego is intact, thank you."

"Well that figures, I suppose. It's quite large, would take a lot to damage it. I thought a bullet from a tank's gun would do the trick though."

"They're not bullets, they're shells."

"So more than one bullet, got it."

"Um, hope I'm not interruptin' anything?" Ezra's voice wafted from the entrance.

Ruth glanced over to see the girl standing with her hip cocked to the side. She was fidgeting with the sweater in her hands. "Hey, Ez, yeah, I'm ready." Ruth bounced off the couch. "But I thought you'd still be busy for a few minutes?"

"Oh, your dad said I could leave for the day since I'd finished what he had in mind for now. He's usually more worried about specific tasks bein' completed then the exact amount of time I'm scheduled. Plus, he seemed a bit distracted with somethin' he was workin' on."

Ruth nodded as she grabbed her purse, calling, "Adios," over her shoulder to David as she went. She followed Ezra out to her car, asking how she was.

"Well..." Ezra responded slowly as she got into her car.

Ruth followed suit, turning to look curiously at Ezra

as she fastened her seatbelt.

"I'm okay, I guess," Ezra said quietly.

"Still kind of freaking out about everything?"

"Yeah, and I've started feelin' queasy, and I'm worried it's goin' tah affect my work." Ezra turned the car on and slowly backed out of the driveway.

"Your child is more important than your job. Besides, my dad will understand."

"Yeah, but my work is like the one steady thing in my life right now. It's the one constant that makes sense. My life is changin', my body is changin', my boyfriend left, I'm scared and frustrated, and now I'm afraid I won't even be able tah keep goin' to work like normal."

"Not everything is changing," Ruth hoped her words would provide some comfort even though she really had no idea what to say. "You get to stay in your home with your loving family and the pregnancy will only last for nine months. Then your body will start transitioning back to normal."

"And then what?" Ezra's nervousness was as clear in her voice as it was written on her face.

"What do you mean?"

"I don't even know what I'm goin' tah do with my own baby! Am I goin' tah keep it, give it up? I have my whole life in front of me."

"Well, you don't have to decide that now."

"But *how* do I decide that ever?"

"Pray about it, I guess." Ruth shifted uncomfortably in her seat.

"I have been, but I'm too emotional tah hear the answer."

"Read your Bible."

Ezra gave a soft, frustrated sigh. "Don't ya think I have been?" she asked shakily.

"I'm sorry, I just don't know what to say," Ruth said, voice barely above a whisper. "I've never been in your situation, I don't know what you're going through. I'm just here to help if you need anything."

"Thank you." The words were almost a whisper as well and after Ezra spoke them, the car went quiet. After a few minutes, she turned on the radio, presumably to break the silence until they made it to her house.

~ Chapter 20: Worrying ~

Ezra's mom greeted them at the door and asked Ruth if she wanted anything to drink. Ruth graciously declined with a smile, and Ezra said they were going up to her room.

"Okay, dears," her mother said before reaching into the cupboard for something.

Ruth followed Ezra to her room in silence. When they made it to her bedroom, Ezra settled onto the bed while Ruth snuggled into a bean bag placed in a corner of the room.

"So..." Ruth said after a few minutes of quiet had awkwardly passed.

"So."

"So, what do you like to do for fun?"

"Uh, I like tah..." Ezra paused for a moment, "Draw, read, paint, play with the computer."

"Oh? What sort of stuff do you draw?"

"Horses mainly," Ezra responded.

"Can I see?" Ruth asked.

Ezra nodded and went to her desk. She rifled through a few papers before she produced a scrapbook with stuck-in pages sticking out at all angles. She sat on the bed, her gaze moving up to Ruth in question, as if asking her to sit beside her.

Ruth gave a small nod and quickly popped up from the bean bag to settle on the bed next to Ezra.

Ezra flipped open the scrapbook on her lap and started to flip through the pages slowly, tilting the book toward Ruth. The drawings were just as Ezra had said, mainly sketches of horses, but there were some other animals spattered in the sketches such as dogs, cats, and birds. There were random drawings of other things that must have struck Ezra's interest enough for inspiration, such as leaves, roses, waterfalls, and trees. There were also a handful of drawings of people, though it was plain to see her skill in that area was less refined.

Occasionally, Ezra would make a comment about one of the pictures, or Ruth would say something complimentary, but for the most part they were quiet. Ruth was glad they had an activity for a while though, it was better than sitting and staring at each other. Her mind was already moving, trying to think of an activity that they could do once they got through the scrapbook.

About three/fourths of the way through the scrapbook, Ruth's cell began to ring. "Just a minute," Ruth said quietly as she pulled her phone out to look at it.

Ezra gave a small nod, her long blonde hair bobbing the slightest as she did so.

'Dad' was the name of the caller displayed across the screen. "Just a minute, I should take this." Ruth got up and hit answer. "Hello?" she asked into the mouthpiece as she stepped into the hallway. Maybe he had forgotten that she was going to Ezra's and was just wondering where she was.

"Hello, hon," his voice was low and concerned. "I don't want you to be worried, but I was calling to let you know that I'm taking your Grandfather to the hospital."

"I'm sorry, what?" It didn't quite make sense to Ruth. Sure, he was sick, but he wasn't supposed to end up in the hospital. He was supposed to quickly recover and be at the barn, smiling brightly, the next day.

"I'm going to take him to the hospital. He called me and asked me to bring him something for dinner. He sounds awful, and at his age it's not worth the risk. I'm in the car now, headed that way with your brother. I'm sure we'll have to drag him there kicking and screaming, but that's just what we'll do if needed."

"Should I meet you there?" Her heart felt as if it was caught in her throat.

"No, I don't think that's necessary. I will call and let you know of any important developments. I just think he needs to get checked out."

"Okay, Dad. Thanks for letting me know."

"You have fun with Ezra, I promise I'll let you know if it's anything serious. Don't worry, I'm sure it's just a cold or something and he just needs some rest and fluids. There's nothing you can do. Really, we're just taking him in to get checked out at this point."

"Okay, Dad."

"Talk to you later, sweetie. Bye."

"Goodbye." She hung up after he did and then shuffled back into the bedroom where Ezra was still sitting on the bed, the scrapbook in her lap.

She was staring at one of the pictures, tilting it slightly this way and that as she evaluated it with critical eyes. Judging by the frown tugging the edges of her lips she was unhappy with the drawing for some reason. She looked up as Ruth approached her. "Hey, everything okay?"

"Not really, but my Dad said he'd keep me updated."

"What's goin' on? What'd Peter say?"

"Malachi's going to the hospital."

Ezra's face fell. "Oh no. I'm sorry, Ruth."

Ruth gave a slight shrug. "Thanks, not much anyone can do right now though. Just going to have to wait and see what the doctor's say."

"Do ya need me tah take you to the hospital?"

"Not at this time. Dad said he'd let me know of any

developments, so maybe later, but right now we can just chat if you'd like." She plopped dejectedly onto the bed next to Ezra.

Ezra wrapped an arm around Ruth in comfort.

Ruth sighed, setting her hands in her lap as she turned her attention back to Ezra's drawings and tried not to think about Grandpa Malachi.

The rest of the evening seemed to drag on. Ezra was pleasant enough, but Ruth had difficulty coming up with small talk when her mind was focused on Malachi and what may or may not be happening at the hospital. How could she think of mundane, unimportant things when something so important was happening that very night? She should be with her grandfather.

Her father was right though, there wasn't anything she could do. That didn't help take her mind off it.

She tried to focus on Ezra for the time being as much as she could. Ezra needed her help as well, she was going through her own crisis. As they finally picked out a movie and sat down to watch it on Ezra's laptop, Ruth let her mind stray and found herself praying for her grandfather more than watching the movie. She almost felt a sensation of relief when the night was over.

~ Chapter 21: Grandpa ~

Ruth didn't sleep well that night. Her brother and father were home by the time she made it back and questioned them on everything. There wasn't much more for her to know, though. He had pneumonia and they forced him to go to the hospital because, as her father suspected, when they went to check on him, they found that his health was decreasing quickly.

He had been somewhat resistant, but considering his weakened condition, he couldn't put up much of a fight, verbally or otherwise, so they had him loaded into the car and swiftly had him at the hospital. The doctors had checked him over, asked a few questions, ran some tests, and had a diagnosis quite promptly.

They hooked him up to an IV and started a regimen of medication. They said it was good he had been brought in, in most cases pneumonia was curable, but elderly patients were at an increased risk. They should have more information within a day or so, when they could gauge how he was reacting to the treatment.

Ruth hoped and prayed everything would be okay,

but she felt helpless and it felt almost wrong for her to go to bed and fall asleep when her grandfather was in the hospital. Shouldn't she be doing something? Shouldn't she be helping in some way, not just sleeping her time away? She spent most of the night tossing and turning, her thoughts never drifting far from her worries. Ruth was relieved when morning finally came.

She made it to the breakfast table before it was even seven o'clock. There wasn't any food at the table so Ruth rummaged through the kitchen to find some cold cereal. She was shooed out with her treasures by Sophia, who entered a few minutes after her. Sophia did not appreciate people being in her kitchen.

Ruth sat at the table and started to make headway with her bowl of cereal. Grandpa, that was all she could think about. He made it easier to adjust to everything. She had a wonderful father but he was often busy with work. David was just David, she wanted to punch him as much as hug him sometimes. Brothers. Ezra and Marie were her only friends, and those were new relationships. She needed her grandfather to make every day seem a little lighter, a little easier to deal with.

Besides, he was just starting to teach her his apparently vast expounds of horse sense. She told herself she was likely stressing and worrying for nothing, spending too much time thinking about something she could do nothing about. After she finished with her breakfast, she dropped her plates off in the kitchen and headed to the barn.

Before she knew it, she found herself in the hayloft, leaned up against a bale of hay, crying. She muttered prayers to God, finding some comfort in the act itself. After a few minutes, her tears lessened and she realized she was crying about more than her grandfather.

Everything was spiraling around her. She felt more out of control of her life than she ever had. She had lost her friends, her home, her town, her school, and now she was scared God was going to start taking her family away from her, too. Had she done something to deserve this? What had she done to cause her life to start crumbling all around her?

Though she knew the thoughts were coming from her overactive emotions, for a split second she felt maybe the world would be better off without her. If God was really punishing her for something, maybe those around her would be better off if she wasn't around. At least then she wouldn't be putting them in danger of punishment.

She shook her head and prayed harder. There was nothing she could think of that would have made her deserve this. She was far from perfect but she did her best, and after all, she was only human. She knew God understood that, Jesus had been one himself.

After some time, Ruth found it hard to even pray, she didn't know what to pray for. She just felt alone and hurting. What did she want from God? She just wanted the pain to go away. She wanted to know if she was being punished, if she had done something wrong. She pulled out her phone and began to scroll through her Bible app.

She was shortly in Matthew, chapter eleven, and she began reading. The verse that stuck out to her first was verse twenty-eight, "Come unto me, all ye that labour and are heavy laden, and I will give you rest" (KJV). She continued reading through to the end of the chapter, "Take my yoke upon you, and learn of me; for I am meek and lowly in heart: and ye shall find rest unto your souls. For my yoke is easy, and my burden light" (KJV).

She leaned further back against the hay bale and re-read the verses several times. Then she tried to figure out why she was trying to carry the pain alone. Yes, it hurt and she was worried with her grandfather being in the hospital, but she wasn't alone. God had never let her down, and her brother and father were experiencing it right there with her.

She closed her eyes and began to pray again, asking God to take the pain from her, to ease her burden, to ease her fear. Slowly, she felt as if a weight was being lifted from her. By the time she heard her father calling from the barn aisle, she felt enveloped in a haze of comfort.

"Yeah?" she called down.

"We're going to visit your grandfather in the hospital, would you like to come with?"

She jumped up. "Of course!" she hollered back as she scrambled down the ladder. When she made it down the ladder, she squeezed her father in a tight hug.

He hugged her back tenderly and then wrapped an arm about her shoulders, turning the two of them back toward the driveway. "Come on," he said gently, "David is waiting in the car."

The car was idling not far from the barn. David was indeed waiting for them, sitting in the passenger seat. Peter gave Ruth one more comforting squeeze before releasing her. She scrambled into the back seat.

Ruth fiddled with her phone on the drive to the hospital, trying to find whatever she could to distract enough to keep her mind off her grandfather's situation. She let go of a soft, pent-up sigh of worry once they made it into the hospital parking lot and climbed out of the car.

She took a hard, deep breath and sent another quick prayer to heaven as she followed her father and brother into the hospital.

~ Chapter 22: Too Stubborn To Be Sick ~

They checked in at the front desk, Ruth's father writing down their names. He led them to Grandpa Malachi's hospital room.

Ruth's grandfather was lying on the hospital bed, looking rather weak, but a grin was on his face. He had his Bible propped up in front of him, leaning against the pull-out tray over the bed, and he seemed somewhat amused about something.

"Hey, old man," Peter said as he approached the bed.

"Hey, you young whipper-snapper," Malachi greeted.

"Terrorizing the nurses or something? What's that grin all about?"

He chuckled softly and shrugged. "Oh, far from it. I'm helpin' them."

"Oh no," David groaned softly in mock horror.

Grandpa laughed and shook his head. "You all are so distrustin' of me."

"It's not that we are distrusting," Ruth's father said. "We do trust you. We trust you to be you and cause trouble wherever you go."

Malachi shook his head. "She was just askin' me
some things about how I was feelin', and seemed surprised
by my cheerful answer, which of course opened the door tah
share the love of Christ with her. She seemed a bit confused
by the time she left, can't imagine why, I was quite clear in
what I said."

By the time Malachi finished speaking, they were all
chuckling and shaking their head. "I'm sure you were clear,"
Peter responded as he settled into one of the chairs
positioned to face the bed.

"Oh, I'm not worried about it, I'm sure she'll be back
sooner or later tah take care of me, and I'll clear up any
confusion she might have."

"Or make her more confused," Ruth interjected.

Grandpa gave her a look of exasperation. "Come on
now, when do I ever confuse you?"

Ruth laughed softly. "Grandpa, I'm confused by you
every time I see you."

"Well, that's kinda rude. I'm just a simple old man."

"Old man you may be," Peter cut in, "but simple you
are not. I agree with Ruth."

"As do I," David added.

"You agree with me?" Ruth asked David with a
raised eyebrow. "First time for everything, I guess."

Grandpa let out a loud huff, "All you young people,

no respect fer your elders!"

"I respect you, Grandpa!" Ruth protested.

"I do as well," her father said. "I just also know you well enough to know the truth."

"And what truth might that be?"

"That you are a little bit crazy, and things aren't always as simple as they first appear when it comes to you."

"Well that's just somethin' I learned from you. How tah be shifty."

Peter laughed heartily. "I hardly think my ability to have meaning hidden in my words which cause people to still be thinking two hours later, is half as refined as yours."

Malachi shrugged with a smirk, his shoulders pushing against his pillow. "Comes with experience."

"So, you're saying when I'm an old fart like you, I'll be as good at it as you?" Peter chuckled.

Malachi shook his head again. "Such disrespect," he responded teasingly. "And no, probably not. You've always been so hard-headed, takes yah longer to learn because of that." He smirked at his son, his blue eyes sparkling despite his illness.

"So, that's where David gets it from," Ruth piped up.

David snorted. "You're twenty times worse than me."

"I may have grown up as the younger sister of the expert, but I certainly haven't surpassed you."

"Do we have another sibling or something? Because if there is someone that is more stubborn and hard-headed than you, I have yet to meet them."

"Alright, you two, we aren't here to hear your sibling rivalry," Peter cut in.

"Yeah, David," Ruth quipped.

"You started it."

"Hush," Ruth said, putting her finger up to her mouth as she shushed him. "Dad said you need to be quiet."

"We both need to be."

"That's correct," Peter cut in.

A short silence ensued and that's when a soft snoring was heard. Ruth looked down and noticed that somewhere amidst the back and forth, her grandfather had drifted off. She smiled softly and looked up to her brother and father.

Her father's brow was creased slightly in worry still, but he was smiling at his father.

David wasn't smiling, but something about his eyes was readable as being at peace with the fact the elderly man was sleeping. or maybe it was the knowledge God was going to take care of him.

"We should go," Peter said quietly.

David and Ruth both nodded and they streamed out of the hospital room.

"Anyone hungry?" Ruth asked after they made it a

few yards from the room.

"It's a bit early, but I suppose I could eat," Peter
noted.

"I could, too," David added.

"So, where are we going?"

"I don't know, maybe we'll go to a sit-down
restaurant. Spend some time together. Then we can swing
back to the hospital on our way out of town and see Grandpa
again."

"Okay, sounds good," David said.

Ruth didn't bother adding anything, figuring the
decision was mostly made, and she didn't have any
objections anyway.

After a rather uneventful lunch, they did stop by the
hospital again to check on Grandpa Malachi, but he was still
out like a light so they headed home. The ride home was
fairly quiet, whether from nerves or relief, Ruth wasn't sure,
but she had a lot on her mind. She headed to the barn as soon
as they were parked. She was surprised to run into Marie,
who was mucking out a stall. "Oh, hi!"

"Hey there," Marie greeted back shyly.

"Are you here to help with the chores in return for
time with the horses again?"

Marie nodded. "Ezra's been helpin' me out and
lettin' me know what tah do."

"Makes sense, she's super nice. You want to ride a horse today?"

"I was hopin' to," Marie responded somewhat bashfully.

"Do you know which horse?"

"Maybe Mirage? Since she's so well trained? If that's okay."

"I don't see why not. How much do you have to do yet?"

"I don't know, have one more stall tah muck and then I'm supposed to find Ezra. Not sure if I'll be free after that, or if she'll have more for me tah do."

"Okay, well come find or text me when you're free then."

"Of course, will do!"

Ruth nodded and headed to the hayloft with her phone. She had a sudden sense of loneliness and decided to call her best friends from Wisconsin. Neither Jill or Charlene answered, and she wasn't in the mood to talk to either of the boys.

She slumped against a haybale and started to play with her phone, but the heat got to her all too quickly and she soon headed back into the house. She flopped onto the couch and closed her eyes.

~ Chapter 23: Giddy Marie ~

Ruth woke to someone gently shaking her shoulder and she groggily opened her eyes to find Marie peering down at her. A slight flush filled the girl's somewhat chubby cheeks and she pulled away.

"Wha-?" Ruth muttered.

"Uh, I'm um, done. And you had asked me tah come find you when I finished with the chores and was ready tah ride." She shrugged in mild embarrassment though a smile was twitching at the corners of her lips. "And I'm ready."

"Right," Ruth mumbled, stretching on the couch before rolling off, setting her feet on the floor and standing slowly. "Okay, let's go." She rubbed her eyes.

Ruth pulled her cell off the coffee table next to the couch and checked the time. She'd napped for almost two hours. Man, it hadn't felt that long. Maybe it was just the stress of Grandpa being sick that was causing her to feel so tired. She followed Marie out of the house and across the driveway to the barn.

Mirage and Embera were tied in the aisle, saddled and ready to ride.

"I assumed you wanted tah ride Embera, I hope that's okay? Ezra helped me get them ready."

"Of course, and yes, she is who I wanted to ride. Thank you."

"Great!" Marie replied before going to Mirage and untying her lead rope. The mare nudged Marie's hand gently, sniffing at it as she did so.

Ruth smiled and untied Embera's lead. "So what, are we going for a trail ride?"

"I was hopin' so?"

"Maybe we should start with some ground work first, make sure the horses are in the right mindset," Ruth said, somewhat skeptical as she looked at the young chestnut mare beside her. She felt pretty comfortable taking Mirage right out on the trail but the young mare, not so much. Besides, she felt that her grandfather would do groundwork first, and he was better with horses than most anyone she had seen.

Marie nodded but the look on her face seemed somewhat unsure and Ruth understood why when the girl spoke up. "Um, what do we do? Just what we did in the trainin' course?"

"Yes, that sounds good. Let's go to the indoor arena, it will be a bit cooler. Don't want to be dying from the heat before we ever get onto the trail." Ruth led the way toward the arena with Embera. *Don't really want to die from the heat period.'*

"Okay, that sounds fine," Marie agreed, following Ruth with Mirage.

They passed Victoria as they walked toward the arena, and saw a scowl on her face.

"Are you alright?" Ruth asked, unsure why she was asking.

Victoria cast them an angry glare but kept stomping down the aisle and disappeared into the tack room.

Ruth gave Marie a slight shrug and the two girls continued walking toward the indoor arena, grabbing lunge whips on the way. As they passed the outdoor arena, Ruth noticed that Victoria's instructor had set up a folding chair and was sitting outside the arena, a course set up within it. Ruth figured Victoria's mood had something to do with that, though how, she couldn't say.

After making it to the indoor arena, they started to play with the horses on the ground as Malachi had taught in the class he instructed. The horses actually seemed to enjoy themselves and after a few minutes they were responsive and attentive to Marie and Ruth respectively.

"Alright, do you think they're ready?" Ruth said, somewhat nervous. She felt Marie was her responsibility at the moment and didn't want to push things too fast.

"Finally!" Marie said giddily. Ah, there was her

peppy side coming out again. "I think they've been ready fer *hours*," she said with obvious exaggeration in her tone.

"We haven't even been out her for hours."

"Long enough, let's hit the trail!"

Ruth chuckled and nodded, heading to open the gate. She gave Embera a few encouraging strokes before mounting. She was usually calmer and gentler with the horses, but her normal amount of pressure tended not to phase Embera, so she'd started applying more pressure when praising the mare, to get the excited mare to pay attention.

The Arabian was fairly calm from the groundwork and she flicked an ear toward Ruth, her head turned to the side, a large brown eye on Ruth as if confirming it was okay to mount. Ruth did just that and felt the usual thrill of sitting upon a horse. She sucked in a deep, calming breath and looked toward Marie.

The girl seemed ready to go, a bright smile plastered across her face. "Let's hit the trail!" she exclaimed.

Mirage had both ears turned back toward Marie, her head half down, eyes partly lidded. The blue roan really was a beautiful mare, Ruth noted. So was Embera. So was every horse at the barn. So was, perhaps, every horse she had seen throughout her life. Horses were just beautiful. Period.

"Alright, let's go," Ruth said, raising her energy and giving the horse a light squeeze with her legs, encouraging the mare into a walk. She'd barely applied pressure before the Arabian starting walking and Ruth turned the mare toward the trail she usually took.

In a few moments, Marie had pulled up beside Ruth on Mirage with an elated smile. "Alrighty! This is fun!" Marie said enthusiastically.

Ruth chuckled slightly and nodded. "Yes, I agree, but we haven't actually hit the trail yet."

"But we are out in the country, on beautiful horses, going on a trail ride! Awesome!"

Ruth chuckled again. "Yep. That pretty much sums it up."

Marie responded with a light giggle but the girls went quiet as they rode past the outdoor arena.

The tension in the air as the trainer shouted at Victoria about her posture was palpable.

Marie and Ruth exchanged glances and didn't speak again until they had made it a few yards down the wooded trail.

"So..." Marie was the first to speak, "that was kinda awkward." There was the usual laughing tilt to her voice and Ruth nodded in response.

"A little, but she's training for competition. Usually how things go I'd assume."

"She seems really stressed."

"Yeah," Ruth wasn't sure what else to say.

"I suppose that's also how things usually go," Marie tittered.

"I suppose so. Never actually been in a competition myself," Ruth admitted.

"Really? That surprises me. I mean, why not?"

"I don't know, perhaps because I never had a horse of my own. But I really enjoy building a relationship with the horse, even without the competition."

"I guess I can understand that."

"I mean, not everyone that has a dog takes their dog to shows. Or everyone that has a cat, for certain." She chuckled and Marie joined in with her own giggle. "I mean, I just don't think you need to be in a competition to appreciate your animals. Maybe I will at some point, but I love horses without the crowds or ribbons just fine."

"Maybe people just get bored."

"I don't." Ruth shrugged. "I mean, I like learning new things with horses and I'm just as competitive as the next girl, but I love horses for horses. They are beautiful, intelligent, affectionate, amazing creatures, and if you view them as a pet, which is why most people have them, then you don't need to accomplish anything with them."

"Isn't it a business fer your dad though?"

"Well, yeah, but he just doesn't want it to drain his

funds. It's not like it's how we make a living. He has his own business that supports us. This is a dream of his and he wants it to support itself as much as possible."

"Ah, that must be nice."

"What?"

"Not to have to worry about the money."

"Yeah, I suppose. I mean, we still have our issues, but yes, I know running a horse ranch can be tight. And it's nice that we don't have to worry about that as much as some." Ruth shifted slightly in her saddle to look at Marie.

The girl's dark, short brown hair was fluttering lightly in the wind as she focused ahead on the trail. Her and Mirage were almost side by side with Ruth and Embera, though she was following a little behind. Ruth was glad she had chosen this wide trail that allowed enough room for both horses at once. Marie looked back to Ruth and smiled.

The two girls were silent for a few minutes, just listening to the birds, hearing the hoofbeats, and Ruth in particular, tried to ignore the heat that was causing beads of sweat to trail annoyingly down her back. Then Ruth broke the silence. "So, what about you? You ever been in competitions?"

Marie shook her head. "No, we don't really have enough money to. And I've never had my own horse or any horse to compete on, either."

"Well if it's something you want to do maybe you will be able to here in the future."

"I hope so! That would be awesome! Though, I just enjoy bein' with the horses, too, it's not somethin' I have tah have." The excitement that light up Marie's face at the thought though made Ruth smile.

Hopefully they would be able to help her with that, seemed like a dream of hers.

The girls continued to chat about different things throughout the ride. The horses seemed rather content at the walking pace they tended to stay at. Sometimes it was nice just to enjoy the quiet and the horses.

They made it back to the barn a couple hours later and Ruth noticed her stomach was grumbling wildly. "Hey, when is your mom supposed to pick you back up?"

"I'm supposed to call her later."

"Ah." Ruth pulled her phone from her pocket. It was almost dinnertime. "Want to stay for dinner? I doubt my dad would mind."

"Oh, I'd love to! But I should call my mom first."

"Of course," Ruth replied, dismounting as they reached the edge of the barn aisle.

Butterscotch was in her stall now and she whinnied as the girls reached the barn, a hint of loneliness in her pitch. Suddenly an orange and white dash blurred past and in a few moments, the fluffy Amerigo was stretched out on top of the stall door. Butterscotch moved forward and sniffed at the kitten who started purring loudly.

Ruth chuckled.

"Aww! That's so cute!"

"Yeah, animals have their moments for sure."

Marie chuckled and then texted her mom before the two girls went to work removing the horses' tack. When they were leading the horses back out to pasture, Marie's phone dinged.

Ruth glanced over her shoulder at her but then focused on Embera. She let the mare free and as she turned back, Marie was frowning slightly.

"Mom said she's goin' to come get me, wants me home for dinner. But thank you, maybe next time?"

"Sure, I look forward to it."

"Awesome!" Marie suddenly gave Ruth a hug and then giddily walked past and headed down the barn aisle.

Ruth chuckled, shaking her head and closing the gate behind her as she headed toward the house. She liked Marie, hopefully the girl would keep coming around.

~ Chapter 24: Home and Loneliness ~

"So, how'd it go with Marie?" Peter's voice interrupted the silence looming over dinner.

"Hm?" Ruth asked, then her mind caught up with the question. "Oh, right. Um, it was great! She's really nice, thanks for letting her volunteer."

"I'm not going to complain if people offer free labor. Besides, the horses need ridden anyway, so it's a win-win."

"Yeah, plus it gives me someone to ride with."

"You could ride with me," Peter added.

"That would be awesome!" Ruth chimed. "Oh, and when Grandpa gets better, when is the next horse class going to be?"

"I don't know exactly. Let's see when he starts feeling better and we'll talk about it then."

"I can go for a ride, too," David added. "I mean, I might not have much experience with horses but it can't be that hard, Ruth does it."

Ruth rolled her eyes at her brother. "You wish you could do all the things I can do."

"Just because I choose not to do them, doesn't mean I

can't."

"Mhm, you *choose* not to do them. Right. We'll go with that."

David rolled his eyes and pecked at the casserole that Sophia had prepared them for dinner, but a smile was tracing his lips. He could be a pain sometimes but he apparently enjoyed the bickering he and Ruth engaged in.

"By the way, Caleb is going to be bringing his horse over tomorrow around ten A.M. Can you be there and ready to help him unload when he gets here?"

Ruth looked up at her father. Caleb? Really? "Of course, Dad." Apparently, her compliant answer didn't hide the dissatisfaction in her face because her father chuckled.

"If you need help, Ezra and Devin will be around."

"Working on something else I'm sure," she muttered.

"Most likely, but I'm sure they can spare a few minutes if you need them. By the way, I need you to mow the lawn tomorrow as well."

Ruth sighed and glanced at David. "Is he going to mow the lawn ever?"

David laughed heartily. "I mowed the lawns for years, about time you try to catch up."

"You get paid to do it, hon," her father spoke up. "If you don't want to, you can just go broke."

Ruth laughed. "Wow, you make that option sound so

alluring."

"Well it's how life is, work or starve," David chimed in.

Ruth rolled her eyes at her brother. "I know, oh wise one. We grew up in the same house, remember? I have been taught the same lessons as you."

"Well you're sitting there complaining about having the opportunity to make money while I'm happy to have a job."

Ruth chuckled and poked a fork at her food. "I am happy," she muttered, but as she said it a small part of her wondered if she meant it.

"Well good," Peter chimed in. "I expect a smile on your face as you pop out tomorrow to do your chores then."

She laughed again and looked up at her father. "Of course, Dad. Always bouncy, you know me!" But as she said it, she felt a twinge of guilt, as if she had lied, because she realized that she was feeling less bouncy than usual, a lot less happy. She loved horses, she was even learning to enjoy country life. Yet, everything was so foreign to her and she was feeling more and more broken each day.

She had good moments, moments that she was happy. Riding with Marie made her happy, being in solitude with the horses or even in the hayloft sometimes made her feel peaceful. But more and more she was feeling this weight on her shoulders, this sense that she was lost and had no idea who she was anymore or what anything around her was.

She missed her friends. Marie and Ezra were nice but they weren't Charlotte or Jill. And all those friends from Wisconsin that were supposed to call her, that she gave her number to, they didn't call. She had to call even her close friends and it was luck of the draw whether they would answer or not.

She felt more alone than she ever had, even with her family, even while she thought she was making new friends. She felt that she couldn't talk to anyone about her true feelings. Not without sounding childish or ungrateful. She missed Wisconsin. She missed being somewhere she knew people and the things around her.

She missed being where she didn't feel she was going to melt from the heat the moment she stepped outside. She missed the scent of pine. She missed the state she'd grown proud of. A state where she knew the state animal and the state bird. She missed being around people she understood that grew up in a culture she was used to. She missed her friends. She missed her old life.

Ruth didn't realize how caught up she was in her own thoughts until she was startled by her brother rising from the table. She fidgeted a bit, tucking a strand of dark hair behind an ear as David deposited his dishes into the kitchen.

"Hey, David!" Peter called.

Ruth glanced up.

"Speaking of chores around the house, you can clean the dishes from dinner!"

Ruth smiled softly as she heard her brother grumbling something from the kitchen.

Peter grinned at her, he'd obviously heard the muttering as well, but David didn't really have a choice and he knew it.

Yet, being David, he still tried to get out of it. "But I don't get paid for it like Ruth!"

"Ruth doesn't get paid for dishes or simple home chores either. She gets paid for ranch work. You're not getting paid to just clean up the house, that's your job as my kid!"

There was no response from David.

Ruth gave her father another smile and then stood to deposit her own dishes into the kitchen where David was unloading the dishwasher.

"Don't know why I have to do this by myself."

Ruth shrugged. "Got a problem with it, you'll have to talk to dad, I guess." She wasn't going to help just because he was complaining. It wouldn't take him that long.

"Yeah, well go enjoy your free time while I slave away."

"Oh my goodness, you're such a baby! Whatever happened to being glad that you have work to do?"

"I get paid at my other job."

"And you get fed here."

"That's right," their father's voice came from behind them.

Ruth spun around to smile at her father and used the opportunity to sneak out of the kitchen before she did get sucked into some chore, dishes or other.

She made her way to her bedroom, tried to call Charlene and then Jill. After no luck, she tried to get in touch with James and Drake as well. Nothing. She sighed, collapsing back on her bed and staring at the ceiling.

"I don't understand," she murmured, eyes on the ceiling, mind on God. "I mean, I don't want to complain, I just... I feel so empty. Why couldn't we have these things in Wisconsin?"

Her mind drifted to Grandpa and how it was good for him to have his family close when he was sick like he was. And then she thought of her father and how he probably felt more at home here.

She sighed to herself, her eyes tracing the patterns of paint on the ceiling. She probably shouldn't say anything, she was being selfish. She felt guilty. But she was hurting, she felt lonely. She pulled her phone out and started rifling through social media. Who was she supposed to talk to?

    She set her phone back down and curled up onto her bed, clutching at her blanket and closing her eyes. No one could complain if she let out a little grief in the privacy of her room she thought as she let the feelings of loneliness break through and tears began to roll down her cheeks. She missed home. Could she really be faulted for that?

~ Chapter 25: Kings and Diamonds ~

Ruth woke the next morning to a knocking on her door.

"Ruth?" It was her father.

"Yeah, dad?"

"You need to get up, sweetheart. Caleb is going to be here in thirty minutes."

Ruth groaned and rolled out of bed, still in her clothes from the night before. She must have fallen asleep while she was sulking. "Okay, dad. I'm up," she called to him as she moved to her dresser and pulled out an outfit of jeans and a t-shirt. First things first, she needed to shower.

Ruth tried to get ready quickly but it was fifteen minutes past when Caleb should be there before she finally made it out the door. She didn't usually bother with her makeup but felt since she was helping a new customer get settled in, she should put in a little effort.

She didn't see any vehicles that looked as if they would belong to Caleb in the driveway so she headed straight toward the barn. Devin was taking care of Butterscotch, which was a bit odd since usually Ezra took care of the horse they were rehabilitating. She had a soft spot for the mare.

"Hey, Devin," Ruth greeted him.

He spun around and flashed Ruth a smile. "Hey there, Ruth. How are you?"

Butterscotch nickered a greeting as well.

"Not too bad, Caleb isn't here yet, is he?"

"Nah, but Victoria is. She went to get Winter's Pearl from the pasture."

"Okay." Ruth nodded, offered another brief smile, and headed on down the barn aisle. She wasn't really sure where she was going, she hadn't planned on having to occupy herself until Caleb got there. She had just thought he'd be there by the time she was ready.

She decided to wait in the hayloft, she should be able to hear if he arrived.

Nuzzling up against a haybale, Ruth pulled her phone out of her pocket and begin to play a game she'd downloaded as she waited. She heard some rustling and pulled away from the hay, a bit startled. She expected to see a rat or a mouse, but a white and orange ball of fluff is what greeted her. Amerigo meowed loudly and climbed onto Ruth's lap, emitting his irregular purring as he settled down and stretched out.

Ruth chuckled at the kitten and begin to stroke him

softly. She scratched behind his ears, under his chin, and rubbed the top of his head gently. Stretched out fully on her lap, Amerigo closed his eyes and extended his paws out, curling and uncurling them to paw at the air in enjoyment.

After several minutes, she heard a commotion below and figured she should check it out, might be Caleb. She made her way down the ladder to find it wasn't Caleb at all. She let out a soft sigh of relief. She wasn't looking forward to seeing the blonde teenager again, he wasn't exactly her favorite person in the world.

The man that she found leading a horse out of a trailer wasn't someone she could recall having seen before. He was fairly tall, had to be over six feet, he had dark eyes, dark hair, and a reserved face. The horse he led off the trailer was beautiful though.

It had to be around 15 hands high with a dark chestnut coat, and a flowing flaxen mane and tail. Ruth stared, breathless, as the creature snorted, casting its gaze around as it was led off the trailer.

"I think it's a Black Forest Horse," Ezra said quietly.

Ruth jumped, startled. She hadn't even heard the girl come up. Ruth turned her head and gave her a soft smile, "I'm not sure what breed that is, but he is beautiful."

"That is what that breed is," Ezra indicated the horse with a nod of her head as the man leading him moved up to

Devin.

"So where do I take him?" he asked.

Devin nodded toward Ruth and Ezra, "Have to ask one of them. I was actually on my way to take care of somethin' else." He nodded slightly at the man and then moved off toward the barn with equipment.

Ruth's gaze followed Devin for a bit before it turned to the man as he approached.

"Hello," he greeted pleasantly. "I'm Seth. I am droppin' Kings and Diamonds off fer Caleb Glanden."

"Ah, yes, I'm Ruth and this is Ezra." Ruth said quietly, sparing the shy girl from having to introduce herself. "Please follow me," Ruth turned on her heel and headed toward the barn. Ezra walked beside her as the man followed with Kings and Diamonds.

Ruth led them to the cleaned out stall next to Butterscotch. When Seth removed the halter, Kings and Diamonds immediately moved to the side of the stall to introduce himself to the new horse next to him. Everyone watched quietly as the two sniffed at each other, nostrils flaring with curiosity, ears perked. After a few minutes, they seemed content enough and Butterscotch moved over to stand idly in the center or her stall while Kings and Diamonds moved to the bucket in his stall to suck up some water. Everyone breathed a soft sigh of relief.

If they did end up getting along, Kings and Diamonds might be a nice horse to pair Butterscotch with when she was a little further in recovery.

"Well, it was a pleasure meetin' yah, I need to be off," Seth said politely, nodding his head slightly to them before heading back out to his trailer and truck.

Ruth looked over at Ezra and gave her a pleased smile. "Well, we've got a new horse." She was honestly happy about it because, at the moment, she just got to be around the horse without having to see Caleb. Job done.

"Don't you, uh, need tah go mow the lawn?" Ezra asked softly.

Ruth cast Ezra an amused smile and nodded. "My dad tell you to keep tabs on me? Make sure I get my work done?"

"No," Ezra smiled back though she blushed faintly as she shook her head. "He just went over the work he needed done today and said he was goin' tah have yah meet Caleb to unload his horse and also mow the lawn."

Ruth nodded. "Suuure," she said with a grin before moving off to get the lawn mower and try to mow the lawn in a straight line. Hopefully she'd do a better job of it this time than she did last time.

~ Chapter 26: The Trail Ride ~

After she had finished mowing the lawn in something that somewhat resembled a straight line, Ruth put the mower away and headed inside. She'd planned on working longer after mowing, but she felt oppressed by the burning heat. Even her t-shirt seemed to be too warm for Missouri. She didn't know how people survived in the blazing heat.

Even though she half-expected it, Ruth was a bit surprised when her father asked her to go on a horseback ride with him. She nodded hurriedly and after setting aside the game controller, she followed him out to the barn. "Which horse are you going to ride?"

"I suppose that depends, which horse are you planning on taking out?" he responded.

"Uh," she murmured, her brow creasing as she mulled it over. "Embera, I suppose. I'm starting to get rather attached to her."

"Nothing wrong with that," her father responded, flashing her a wide grin. "May I ask why though?" he asked as they moved into the tack room and found bridles.

"I don't know, she's really intelligent and sweet."

"She's young, has a lot to learn, might be better to start off with a horse like Mirage."

"I know," Ruth said quietly, "and I can, if you want, but I like Embera."

"Of course." Her father nodded. "Embera will be fine, works for me anyway because it leaves Mirage free for me to take."

Ruth flashed him a grin as they two of them walked down the aisle toward the pasture. "So, how do you like Marie?" Ruth asked casually.

"Oh, she seems nice enough. Ezra, too."

"Even though she's pregnant?"

Peter looked down at Ruth and nodded. "That one thing doesn't automatically make her a bad person. People make mistakes. Yes, you need to look at people's actions and not their words, but you also have to understand that people are people, and they are going to make mistakes. They are going to do things they shouldn't, *you* will do things you shouldn't. We all do. You can't judge a person's heart, you need to be careful of people and protect yourself, but you also need to love people. Mind you, I'm not saying she's an angel, but I like her so far. You need to just try to stay in touch with Christ on matters and be careful. She *seems* nice."

Ruth listened silently to her father's words, and nodded in response as they bridled Embera and Mirage.

"Have you seen Victoria training with Winter's Pearl?" her father asked casually as they groomed the horses.

"Yes, it's pretty awesome. Dressage looks neat."

"It can be, takes a lot of dedication and practice. Is that something you want to get into?"

Ruth shrugged as she began to saddle up Embera. "I don't know, maybe. It might be neat to learn. That and everything else."

Her father chuckled. "Everything else?"

"Jumping, Cross Country, Polo, Reining, Vaulting."

Her father shook his head as he finished doing up Mirage's girth. "Vaulting, hm? A bit dangerous, wouldn't you say?"

"Yeah, and I probably couldn't do it anyway since I haven't been in gymnastics or anything so I don't have the flexibility, training, or balance. But it looks so fun! Gymnastics on a horse's back? Color me intrigued."

Her father shook his head, looking over at her from above Mirage's back. "Next you're going to tell me you want to be a cowgirl trick rider."

"You know I never thought of that, but it does sound like a blast!" They both untied their horses and then mounted.

Her father took the lead with Mirage, but as they made it to the wide trail, she pulled up beside him to continue their conversation.

After some time, the talking began to peter off and they soaked up the quiet, just listening to the sound of the horses' hoofbeats. Ruth's thoughts drifted as they rode.

Even though she was extremely glad for being around the horses and able to learn all these new things. Even though she had her family and she was excited about her new friends, it didn't erase the pain of losing her old friends. It didn't make this new place less foreign. And it didn't change that her entire world had been built in Milwaukee and that's where she felt comfortable, that's what she knew.

She felt out of place. Sure, she enjoyed a lot of what living in Ste. Genevieve, Missouri had offered her, but she still felt as if she was a goose swimming with the ducks. Or perhaps a goldfish swimming with the stingrays. She was still in the water, she was still swimming, but what in the world was going on around her? And while she stood out from the crowd, she still felt insignificant.

She mulled over the situation as they rode, sending a few silent prayers to Christ as they went, praying for comfort, guidance, understanding. And praying, most of all, to feel a little less lonely.

She'd become so close to Charlene and Jill, they were people she believed she'd have in her life until the day she died, and she already felt more distant from them.

She would have to learn how to survive without easily accessible taxis, without the people she'd grown up with, without plentiful options of weekend activities. She felt she needed to learn somewhat of a new culture, a new way of speaking, get used to a new level of humidity, a new town, and soon, she realized with a sinking gut, a new school.

Maybe her father would let her be homeschooled. She cast a glance over at her father and frowned slightly. That was doubtful. Her father wouldn't let her run or hide from her fears. Besides, he'd probably think it a good idea to get out and meet new people. He'd push her out of the house to expand her horizons. She shrugged the thoughts off, those were worries for tomorrow.

Today, she was riding with her father down a beautiful wooded trail, with two wonderful horses. Perhaps she just needed to keep her chin up, push on through the hard times, and relish her freed sense of adventure.

About The Author

G.G. Marshall is the author of the <u>Griffin Guard</u> and <u>Horse Haven</u> series as well as Christian non-fiction books. She's an avid lover of reading as well as writing and many other forms of art. She juggles her time between running a business, working part-time, writing, and spending time with her dashing husband, mischievous children, and playful pets. G.G. has lived in Wisconsin, Illinois, Tennessee, and Missouri. She believes in living life to the fullest and can't wait to see where God will take her or what she'll write next. Visit her on her website *www.ggmarshall.com.*

~ **Horse Haven Series** ~

Book 1: <u>No Pizza Delivery</u>

Book 2: <u>Unexpected Allies and Recurring Warts</u>

Book 3: <u>Forward Through the Fertilizer</u>

www.ingramcontent.com/pod-product-compliance
Lightning Source LLC
Chambersburg PA
CBHW071720140626
46557CB00012B/978